A PARENT'S SURVIVAL GUIDE TO MUSIC LESSONS

HELP YOUR CHILD SUCCEED IN MUSIC

Elizabeth Lawrence

BLOOMSBURY

First published 2012 by A&C Black Publishers Ltd, an imprint of
Bloomsbury Publishing Plc.
50 Bedford Square, London, WC1B 3DP
© copyright 2012

ISBN 978 1 4081 606 88

Printed and bound in Great Britain by Latimer Trend Limited
Text © Elizabeth Lawrence 2012
Cover design by Saffron Stocker
Text design by Lynda Murray
Photographs © Fotolia © Shutterstock unless otherwise credited
Other photographs: p 13 © Karla Gowlett; p 65 © Richard Olivier;
p 72 © Tower Hamlets Arts and Music Service (THAMES)
(photographer: Hayley Cook); p 75 © Kiran Ridely

The author and publisher would like to thank the following people for
their generous help during the preparation of the book: Karen Marshall,
Malcolm Pollock, Cyrilla Rowsell, Jacqueline Vann and David Weston.

To see our full range of titles visit **www.bloomsbury.com**

Contents

> ....the woods would be very silent if no birds sang except those that sang best!
>
> Henry Van Dyke

Why do I need this book?

Making music is potentially one of the best experiences we can have as a human being. This guide is for any parent who wants to support their child as they take the first steps of their musical journey and beyond. Even if you don't consider yourself to be musical or if you are on a limited budget, you can still help your child to enjoy making music. In fact, helping your child can be as easy as listening to an impromptu performance or simply reminding them that it's time to practise.

Are all children musical?

Everybody can learn and enjoy playing a musical instrument; it is a question of finding out what suits your child. With the right guidance from a great teacher, motivation from the child and the encouragement and support of their parents, all children can learn how to make music and enjoy it.

Of course, only a small percentage of children go on to make music their career as adults, just as only a small number of children who play sport go on to represent their country in the Olympics or play for a Premier League football team. Regardless of this, everyone has the ability to enjoy and achieve through playing music.

How to use this book

There are many choices that you and your child will need to make when they start taking music lessons. This guide will support you and help you make informed decisions about what is best for your child. It will also help you anticipate and overcome difficulties and make sure that the money you are spending is put to good use. This book is organised into nine sections that cover the most important aspects of learning to play an instrument:

→ Introduction

→ Choosing an instrument

→ Finding a teacher

→ Practising

→ Ensemble playing

→ Problems with progress

→ Exams

→ Performing

→ Useful resources

I'm not musical – can I still help my child?

Research into childhood music making shows that parental involvement is strongly linked to success[1]. Your child needs to know that you are interested in and appreciate their music making. Even if you don't consider yourself to be musical, you can still give your child all the support and encouragement that they need.

Here are some ideas of the ways in which you can get involved:

- share your own musical interests with your child (from pop, rock and metal to classical and traditional music from around the world)

- sing together

- discuss the music that you hear on the radio, on TV or at local events

- make up stories around a piece of music

- explore simple age-appropriate musical games which you can find on the internet or in books with your child (see Useful resources)

- find a teacher who matches your child

- take your child to lessons and rehearsals

- talk to your child about what they have learnt during lessons

- help your child to become organised and to find time for practise

- ask questions about your child's practice or ask them to explain to you what they have learnt (many children enjoy being an expert or knowing more than their parent)

- ask for impromptu performances

- attend school concerts and competitions

[1] *The Social Context of Musical Success: A development account,* Moore, D., Burland, K., Davidson, J., British Journal of Psychology, 2003: 94,529-549.

What are the benefits of music making?

You might have heard of the 'Mozart effect'[2] or other claims about how music can boost a child's IQ. Despite some encouraging findings from academics, the jury is still out on whether making music really does make you 'cleverer'. What is beyond dispute is that your child will acquire invaluable skills through learning an instrument that will help them at school, in sport and in later life[3]. Learning an instrument is also a really fun and sociable activity and many children develop lifelong friendships with other young musicians.

Listening skills and concentration: in order to understand instructions from a teacher or an ensemble leader your child will need to stay focused and listen carefully. Both these skills are also invaluable at school and in later life.

Self-esteem: Learning a new skill, performing and meeting other children who share the same interests all help to build self-confidence.

Social skills and self-confidence: playing music with others gives children plenty of opportunities to develop their social skills in a safe, friendly environment. Taking part in an ensemble is a great way to make new friends with shared interests and to enjoy being part of a group. A recent study by Cambridge University also suggests that regularly playing music in groups may improve a child's ability to empathise with others.[4]

[2]*Music and its Impact,* Prof. G. Bastian, Schott Music, 2000 (a long-term study at Berlin Primary schools). The study is unfortunately only available in German.

[3]*The social context of musical success: A developmental account,* Moore, Burland, Davidson, British journal of Psychology, 2003: 94,529–549

[4]*Long-Term Musical Group Interaction Has a Positive Influence on Empathy in Children,* Rabinowitch, T., Cross, I, Burnard, P. (under review).

UCAS points: if your child chooses to continue with their music education beyond the early years, practical and theory certificates for Grades 6–8 can gain as much as seventy-five valuable UCAS points.

Teamwork: playing in an ensemble gives children an opportunity to learn valuable teamworking skills such as listening, working to goals together, supporting others, learning from experiences as a group and leading.

Coordination: playing an instrument involves controlled finger movements and/or hand and arm movements that, in turn, have been shown by studies to improve hand–eye coordination and fine motor skills over time. These skills are invaluable when it comes to a wide range of activities from handwriting to sports and art.

Verbal skills and non-verbal reasoning: studies have shown that children who have received at least three years of instrumental music training tend to outperform their peers on vocabulary and non-verbal reasoning skills.

Motivation and self-discipline: Tackling new challenges and maintaining motivation are a valuable reminder that difficulties can be overcome and that practice and dedication pay off.

Music has so much to offer young people in terms of creative, social and character development as well as improving coordination and concentration. On top of all that it's great fun!

Peter Desmond Head of Music and Performing Arts, Haringey

Choosing an instrument

There are many practical considerations to be aware of when helping your child to choose an instrument, ranging from your budget to the instrumental teachers available in your area. However, the most important question is: which instrument does my child want to play? This chapter will help you to discuss the topic of choosing an instrument with your child and to help them become aware of the commitment that playing an instrument entails. It will also give you an idea of the parental considerations involved in this decision.

Which instrument do you want to play?

What kind of music do I like listening to?

How motivated are you to learn and practise?

How do I prefer to learn?

Talking to your child about learning an instrument

Which instrument do I want to play?

Some children have a good idea of which instrument they'd like to play from the start and others aren't sure at this early stage. If your child is interested in the idea of music making and would like to explore the different possibilities open to them, there are plenty of ideas on how to introduce your child to different instruments on p11. You could also use the Instrument factfiles to find information on how to play each instrument, playing opportunities, star players and listening tips for the wide range of instruments available for beginners.

As a result of the National Plan for Music Education that was published in November 2011[5], all children aged 5–18 have the opportunity to learn an instrument at school for at least a term, usually at Key Stage 2, through whole-class instrumental teaching organised by the music services/hubs. Lessons will be free in the first instance and your child may also be able to borrow an instrument free of charge from their school or music service/hub.

> Remember that the instrument should be your child's choice and that they will ultimately be more motivated to practise an instrument that reflects their preference.

How motivated am I to learn and practise?

It is worth explaining to your child that they will need to practise their instrument regularly. A good analogy is sport: no footballer just plays matches; they have to train and work on their skills. How does your child feel about this?

What kind of music do I like listening to?

Don't worry if the kind of music your child likes doesn't feature strongly in any of the Instrument factfiles in this chapter. Learning any instrument will give your child the basic transferable musical skills needed to play any genre of music from baroque to punk rock. It is also a great way to appreciate new types of music that your child may not have considered listening to previously.

How do I prefer to learn?

Depending on the learning situation your child may or may not be given the choice between group or individual lessons. If you know that there is a choice on offer it is worth discussing the options with your child and see which of these options they would prefer and why. There is more information and advice about different types of lessons and finding a teacher in Chapter 2.

[5]*The Importance of Music: A National Plan for Music Education*, Department for Education, November 2011

Practical considerations

There are a number of factors that can affect the choice of instrument and music teacher available to you and your child. It is worth being aware of these factors when choosing an instrument and looking for a teacher.

Location

Music services/hubs offer a wide range of instrumental tuition through whole-class teaching at school and through other music groups. If your child is interested in one of the more unusual instruments such as the bassoon or harp, it is worth making some initial enquiries to see which instrumental lessons are on offer at your child's school, local music centre or through local music teachers to avoid any disappointment further down the line.

There are positive signs that the internet may open up new possibilities to children in rural areas. In a recent project initiated by Dumfries and Galloway[6], instrumental lessons were given in schools using video conferencing technology linked with a remote tutor. Warwick University evaluated the project and found that pupils progressed at the same rate as, and In some cases better than, those children tutored in person and the project greatly increased participation rates.

Lifestyle

Playing an instrument requires having a quiet space to practise in that's away from distractions such as TV or siblings. Bear in mind that some instruments create much more noise than others. As well as potentially being less neighbour-friendly, this can create logistical problems if you have more than one child who needs to practise.

> *As both my husband and I work full time, music lessons were only ever feasible at school. Luckily our school has a great music department and all our three kids love their lessons there!*
>
> Alison

Budget

A smaller budget need not be a barrier to music making. If your child is learning an instrument in whole-class lessons at school organised by the local music service/hub they will receive free lessons in the first instance and they may be able to borrow an instrument free of charge from their school or music service/hub. Many music shops, music services/hubs and schools have schemes that offer financial assistance to parents, ranging from help with purchasing instruments to subsidising lessons.

Your commitment

Taking the time to transport your child to lessons and rehearsals, helping them practise in the early stages and attending concerts all take time, effort and commitment. Your input will make a real difference to your child's enjoyment of music lessons. Are you ready for this?

Info point

Some brass and string instruments can be muted and electronic versions of pianos, drum kits and violins are available (there is more information about this in the Instrument factfiles). It is best to check with a prospective teacher first before buying electronic versions of instruments.

[6]*The Importance of Music: A National Plan for Music Education*, Department for Education, Widening Access for Rural Schools in Dumfries and Galloway, case study, p. 52

Introducing your child to different instruments

If your child isn't sure which instrument they'd like to play, there are many ways in which you can introduce them to a wide range of instruments.

- Take your child to outdoor, free music events in your local area.

- Go to family-friendly events such as the Children's Prom at the Royal Albert Hall or events at the Sage, Gateshead, where programming is child-centred and concert etiquette more relaxed.

- Charities such as Music for All run instrument 'taster' sessions both in schools and at other locations. For more information about Music for All, go to www.musicforall.org.uk.

- Many orchestras run community outreach projects such as activities and workshops for children.

- Local libraries and arts centres often offer free musical activities for children.

- Use free music streaming services on the internet such as YouTube, Spotify and last.fm.

- Websites such as Bachtrack (www.bachtrack.com) include listings for children-friendly music events as well as tips for getting children into classical music, information about free or cheap concert ideas for children and links to other useful music information websites.

- Listen to radio stations such as Classic FM and Radio 3 for classical music.

As well as offering whole-class instrumental teaching, many music services/hubs run hands-on sessions at music centres or schools where children can try out several instruments under the guidance of tutors. It's also a good opportunity to ask any questions that you might have about the instrument or teachers. These events are usually extremely popular and are most likely to require advance booking.

Common questions

What age can my child start playing an instrument?

This decision depends entirely on the instrument that your child would like to play and where and with whom they are going to learn. Many children start learning an instrument at around eight or nine years of age, but there are no set rules. Older children can often catch up quickly with their peers who started at an earlier age.

How do I know if my children is ready for formal lessons?

If your child is under five and would like to start playing the violin or the piano, formal lessons should be approached with caution. It is important that your child has the necessary skills to succeed, otherwise the experience might be disappointing and your child could be put off learning an instrument altogether.

The following list serves as a good indicator that your child might be ready for formal lessons. Can your child:

- sit quietly and attentively listen to a story/picture book for ten minutes?
- follow instructions?
- remember the first letters of the alphabet?
- identify patterns?

It is also useful if your child can read simple instructions.

If your child is able to do most of the above they may be ready to start lessons.

Make sure that you find a teacher who is experienced with that particular age group and enjoys teaching younger children. It may also be worth considering a method such as Suzuki that does not initially require your child to read music. Lessons should be short and should last between fifteen to thirty minutes at this age.

Info point

There are now simplified or scaled-down versions of nearly all instruments, making what would otherwise have been a large, cumbersome instrument potentially suitable for younger children. This has increased the choices available for beginners so that instruments such as the double bass, bassoon and oboe can now be learnt from a younger age. It is worth being aware that the simplified instruments, in particular the versions aimed at very young children, will have limited use, and they will need to be replaced as your child grows and progresses on the instrument. Some teachers prefer not to teach on simplified instruments so it is worth checking about this before buying one.

What if my child isn't ready for formal lessons?

If your child isn't quite ready to start formal instrumental lessons, don't worry as this is quite normal. Music is a statutory subject in the National Curriculum from Key Stages 1–3 so your child will already be learning important skills such as singing, listening, performing, composing and appraising at school.

In addition to this, a lot of music services/hubs and other organisations run excellent non-instrumental music lessons that can be a great alternative to formal music lessons. These lessons introduce children to basic musical concepts such as pitch, pulse and rhythm alongside opportunities for expressive and creative development. Some music making courses might also tackle musical notation and learning to read music but are mostly about shared musical experiences and having fun with other children.

> *Music Makers gave my two children a sound understanding of basic musicianship concepts and a great love of music. They couldn't wait to start an instrument and they made rapid progress owing to all they'd learned in Music Makers.*
>
> Richmond Music Trust parent

> *Some children are definitely starting lessons too early. In my private studio I would usually recommend an early years music-making class and suggest to postpone lessons for a year… I try to make lessons fun and engaging and we will do games away from the piano but inevitably progress is very slow. I do often wonder what the parents think or if they are blaming me for their child's lack of progress.*
>
> Rachel, piano teacher

A Music Makers club at Richmond Music Trust. Photo © Karla Gowlett

Teaching methods that are suitable for younger children

Suzuki Method

★ The Suzuki Method of music education is based on the philosophy and teaching methods developed by the Japanese violinist, pedagogue, educator and humanitarian, Dr. Shinichi Suzuki.

★ Dr. Suzuki believed in the great potential of music to enrich children's lives. He developed a method of music education to enable children to play music to their highest possible level of ability. His method was derived from his observation of the ease and facility with which young children learn to speak their own language.

★ All Suzuki students learn and follow the same sequence of material. Each instrument has its own repertoire that has been designed to take a child from the very simplest piece (variations on 'Twinkle Twinkle Little Star') to the Grade 8 level and beyond.

★ Students learn both in individual lessons and in groups.

★ Parents are encouraged to play an active role in the Suzuki Method, particularly in the early years. They are expected to attend lessons, take notes and supervise practice.

★ The usual instruments taught through Suzuki are piano, violin, viola, cello, double bass, recorder, flute, and in rarer circumstances classical guitar, harp and organ.

For more information go to
www.britishsuzuki.com

> *Talent is no accident of birth ... the right environment can change a person with undeveloped ability into a talented one*
>
> Shinichi Suzuki

The Kodály Approach

★ The Kodály Approach is a way of developing musical skills and teaching musical concepts to very young children.

★ The Approach is named after the Hungarian composer, educationalist and ethnomusicologist, Zoltán Kodály, who developed the approach from the 1920s onwards.

★ The main instrument used is the voice, but various tuned and unturned percussion instruments are also used. Songs and singing games are used to provide experience of musical concepts such as pulse, rhythm and pitch and by the use of relative solfa (do, re, mi etc.) and related handsigns. Rhythm syllables are also used.

★ Kodály is not meant to replace instrumental tuition. It builds musicianship skills that are invaluable both for pre-instrumental work and to continue developing skills and understanding concurrent with learning an instrument.

For more information go to
www.britishkodalyacademy.org

> *He who begins life with music will have this reflecting on his future like golden sunshine.*
>
> Zoltán Kodály

Dalcroze Eurhythmics

★ The word eurhythmics means 'good rhythm'. Dalcroze Eurhythmics, or more commonly, Dalcroze, is an approach to understanding music named after its founder Emile Jaques-Dalcroze.

★ The approach uses whole body movement and comprises three main branches: rhythmics, aural training and improvisation. It is widely used in different contexts, from parent and toddler groups to professional musicians.

★ The primary aim of Dalcroze is to make ourselves into a 'musical instrument' using the whole body, the mind and feelings. By exploring and understanding the language of music in this way we can become effective performers and musicians.

★ Dalcroze is a great tool for developing musicianship skills, rhythm and general musicality alongside instrumental lessons.

★ Many other musical and non-musical skills are developed at the same time such as being well co-ordinated, developing a good memory, being able to react quickly, using the body effectively and being able to work on your own or as part of an ensemble.

For more information go to
www.dalcroze.org.uk

> *It is not enough to teach children to interpret music with their fingers ... the important thing is that the child should learn to feel music not only with his ear but with his whole being.*
>
> Emile Jaques-Dalcroze

My child is a teenager; is it too late to start learning?

With the onset of puberty, homework and exam pressures are often combined with an increasing interest in socialising with peers. On the other hand, playing in a band or another ensemble can be a great way to enhance your teenager's well-being, build their social skills and develop their talents, from critical thinking and problem solving to mastering the technical challenges of learning a musical instrument.

Info point

Older children often catch up quickly with peers who started playing at an earlier age. They:

• focus well

• tend to be well motivated

• have more emotional maturity, which can help to interpret music.

I have been told that my child is too young to play a certain instrument

Younger children may not be physically strong enough yet to support their chosen instrument or have hands that are too small to stretch to all the keys. If any of these scenarios are the case it is just a matter of waiting a while and trying again later.

I have been told that my child is not physiologically suited to a certain instrument

Some teachers may advise that your children is unsuited to a certain instrument for physiological reasons, for example they have lips that are considered to thick for the trumpet or too thin for the trombone. They may recommend that your child could potentially make better progress and get more enjoyment from playing an instrument that they are better suited to physiologically.

Other teachers may argue that, while these criteria might have some bearing for those aiming to be a professional musician, they are not essential at this stage of music making and that most of the perceived obstacles can be overcome. If your child is very keen on a particular instrument it may be worth looking for a different teacher and trying out the instrument for a few terms to see how your child gets on.

Budgeting tips

Playing an instrument is not the cheapest hobby, but there are many ways of getting financial assistance. Here are some helpful budgeting tips:

Buy, borrow or rent?

Buying new instruments

The Arts Council's Take it Away scheme **(http://takeitaway.org.uk)** provides interest-free loans via retailers for the purchase of instruments, music accessories and even lessons for five- to twenty-five-year-olds. Parents can apply for a loan between £100 and £2,000. A ten per cent deposit is paid upfront and the remaining costs are then repaid over nine monthly instalments.

The Assisted Instrument Purchase Scheme allows parents of pupils in full-time education at LEA schools receiving instrumental tuition to buy an instrument through their school VAT-free. Contact your school to see whether they are offering this scheme.

When buying an instrument it is a good idea to take a knowledgeable person with you, ideally your child's teacher. Many shops also let you borrow an instrument first so that you can try it out at your or the teacher's home. In addition, most reputable internet retailers will also offer a fourteen-day no-quibbles refund guarantee.

Buying second-hand instruments

Second-hand instruments can be a good option for a first instrument and there are many music shops that sell professionally refurbished instruments. If possible, your child's teacher should help you choose the instrument. If you are thinking about buying a more expensive second-hand instrument, see if you can negotiate a period of a week or so to borrow it and try to show it to an expert to have it independently assessed. This is a normal procedure.

handy tip

Be cautious about buying second-hand instruments on non-specialist internet sites such as eBay. It is hard to judge what condition an instrument is in when buying online and you could end up buying an instrument that is not fit for purpose. Learning to play on a substandard instrument can really put learners off playing and the cost of repairing any faults can really add up.

Borrowing and renting

You may not want to buy an instrument straight away in case your child decides they want to change instruments or pursue an entirely different hobby. Many schools and music services/hubs will let your child borrow an instrument free of charge.

Info point

Most larger music shops also operate rental and rent-to-buy schemes. For some of the more expensive instruments in particular, such as the bassoon or double bass, rental can really make sense. For example, instead of buying a student bassoon for around £1,000 you could start off renting one from around £50 a month.

Bowed strings

What are the most common bowed string instruments?

- violin
- viola
- cello
- double bass

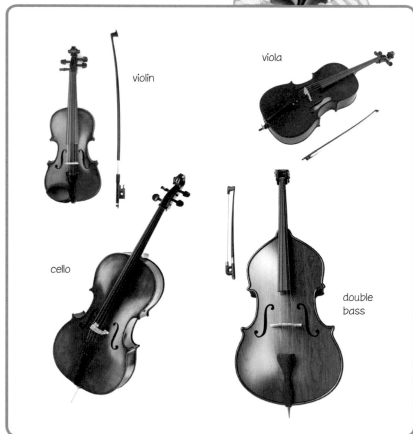

violin

viola

cello

double bass

What styles of music do bowed strings play?

Classical, jazz, pop, folk and country.

Did you know?

One of the most famous instrument makers was the Italian, Antonio Stradivari. His violins were considered to be the Rolls-Royces of the violin world. A Stradivari violin recently sold for nearly £10 million.

Accessories

- cloth for cleaning the strings and instrument body
- replacement strings
- rosin
- shoulder rest (violins, violas)
- black hole (anti-slip grip) or anchor (cello)
- stool and end pin anchor, bow box (double bass)

rosin

Info point

Student adaptations: buy or rent?

All the bowed strings come in smaller sizes so that children don't have to wait until they are big enough to cope with an adult instrument. It is therefore advisable to rent an instrument while your child progresses through the sizes.

Bowed strings

The violin

Popularity

The most popular of the bowed strings.

How to play it

The right arm draws a bow across the strings, the left holds down the strings producing the different notes.

Instrument challenges

Developing a good ear for intonation (tuning), coordination between the left and right hands, fine motor skills, particularly in the left hand.

Starting ages

Possible from three onwards, but usually between six and nine years.

Student adaptations

1/32, 1/8 and 3/4 sizes are available.

Opportunities

Orchestras, chamber music, folk music, jazz and pop.

Listening tips

Johann Sebastian Bach: Double Violin Concerto in D minor

Niccolò Paganini: Caprice No. 24

Django Reinhardt and Stéphane Grappelli: Minor Swing

Pyotr Ilyich Tchaikovsky: Violin Concerto in D major, Op. 35

Instrument price

£150 for a beginner's outfit including bow and case, but if you can invest more it is recommended.

Star players ★ ★ ★ ★ ★ ★

★ Joshua Bell

★ Nicola Benedetti

★ Chris Garrick

★ Maxim Vengerov

★ ★ ★ ★ ★ ★ ★ ★ ★ ★

The viola

Popularity

Less popular, but very much in demand!

How to play it

The right hand draws the bow across the strings, the left holds down the strings producing the different notes.

Instrument challenges

Developing a good ear for intonation (tuning), coordinating the left and right hands, fine motor skills, learning the alto clef.

Starting ages

Determined by hand size. Many children start on the violin then change to the viola when they are ready (see Student adaptations).

Student adaptations

28 cm size violas are now available. This roughly corresponds to a 1/2 sized violin so children can start learning much earlier.

Opportunities

Violas are often in short supply and are a vital part of the classical symphony orchestra and in chamber music. There are no obstacles to playing pop or jazz, but it might be difficult to find a teacher in that particular genre.

Listening tips

Max Bruch: Romanze for Viola, Op. 85

Wolfgang Amadeus Mozart: Sinfonia Concertante for Violin and Viola

Schubert: Sonata for Arpeggione in A Minor

Ralph Vaughan Williams: Suite for Viola and Orchestra

Star players ★ ★ ★ ★ ★ ★

- ★ Yuri Bashmet
- ★ Nobuko Imai
- ★ Emanuel Vardi
- ★ Pinchas Zuckermann

Instrument price

£120 for the cheapest student outfits including case and bow. If you can invest more it is recommended.

Bowed strings

The cello

Popularity

Less frequently played but in great demand.

How to play it

Sitting down, held in front of the body. The right arm draws a bow across the strings, the left holds down the strings producing the different notes.

Instrument challenges

Developing a good ear for intonation (tuning), coordinating the left and right hands, fine motor skills.

Starting ages

Possible from four onwards.

Student adaptations

From 1/8th of adult instruments.

Listening tips

Johann Christian Bach: Suite No. 1, Prelude in G major

Antonín Dvořák: Cello Concerto in B minor

Gabriel Fauré: Elégie, Sicilienne

David Popper: Dance of the Elves, Op. 39

Opportunities

Symphony orchestras and in chamber music. Cellists are often in great demand in school orchestras.

Popular styles

Big repertoire, any genre, but most likely classical.

Star players ★ ★ ★ ★ ★ ★

★ Steven Isserlis

★ Jacqueline du Pré

★ Mstislav Rostropovich

★ Yo-Yo Ma

★ ★ ★ ★ ★ ★ ★ ★

Instrument price

Beginner outfits from around £160, but if you can invest more it is recommended.

Popularity

Not many players due to difficult logistics but in great demand.

How to play it

Sitting on a high chair or standing, the right arm draws a bow across the strings, the left holds down the strings producing the different notes.

Instrument challenges

Developing a good ear for intonation (tuning), coordinating the left and right hands, fine motor skills.

Starting ages

Possible from six onwards on a mini bass.

Student adaptations

Up to 1/4 of adult size; even adult professionals sometimes play on 3/4 basses.

Opportunities

Join an orchestra or a symphonic wind band, or play jazz.

Popular styles

Classical and jazz.

Star players ★ ★ ★ ★ ★

- ★ Ron Carter
- ★ Gary Carr
- ★ Edgar Meyer
- ★ Esperanza Spalding

★ ★ ★ ★ ★ ★ ★ ★ ★

The double bass

Listening tips

George Adams, Clarence 'Gatemouth' Brown, Charles Mingus: Devil Blues

Carl Ditters von Dittersdorf: Double Bass Concerto No. 1 in E major

Vittorio Monti: Csárdás arr. for Double Bass

Camille Saint-Saëns: Carnival of Animals, The Elephant

Instrument price

Second-hand availability is limited; student outfits start around £650, including case and bow.

Plucked strings

What are the most common plucked string instruments?

- ♦ acoustic guitar
- ♦ electric guitar
- ♦ electric bass
- ♦ concert harp

There are also many traditional instruments in the plucked strings family, such as the ukulele, the mandolin, the sitar and the banjo.

What kind of music do they play?

The range of musical genres played by guitars is large and varied. It includes classical, folk, flamenco, jazz, funk, reggae, blues, soul, country and, of course, pop, rock and heavy metal.

The concert harp is mainly used in the classical orchestra. It is a very large and expensive instrument so beginners often start on smaller, folk versions of the instrument.

acoustic guitar

electric guitar

electric bass

Did you know?

The electric guitar was invented in the 1920s and transformed the guitar from a fairly quiet instrument into an 'axe' that can rock entire stadiums! The electric guitar is plugged into an amplifier and with the use of extra equipment such as distortion pedals can produce a variety of sounds, which are impossible on the acoustic instrument.

Accessories

- foot rest for the classical guitar
- plectrum (NB depends on style and instrument)
- electronic tuner (optional)
- amplifier (amp) for electric guitar and bass and effects units (optional)

guitar pedal

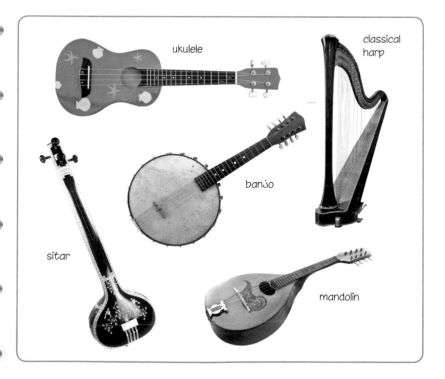

ukulele

classical harp

banjo

sitar

mandolin

Plucked strings

The acoustic guitar

Popularity

Very popular!

How to play it

The left hand holds down the strings to alter the pitch and the right hand strums or plucks the strings.

Instrument challenges

Coordination, fine motor skills and finger agility in both hands.

Starting ages

The guitar is now in the Suzuki syllabus and can be learnt from the age of four but expect progress to be very slow. A more usual age is around eight or nine.

Student adaptations

Comes in 1/4, 1/2, 3/4 size.

Opportunities

Rock and pop bands, jazz ensembles, guitar orchestras, accompanying other instrumentalists.

Listening tips

Isaac Albéniz: Suite Española, Op. 47

Bob Dylan: Blowin' in the Wind

Pat Metheny: Map of the World

Rodrigo y Gabriella: Diablo Rojo

Instrument price

From £80. Make sure the tuning mechnism is sound. At the bottom end of the market there is a huge variation in the quality of instruments.

Star players ★ ★ ★ ★ ★ ★

★ Paco de Lucia

★ Andy McKee

★ Joni Mitchell

★ John Williams

Popularity

Very popular indeed!

How to play it

The left hand holds down the strings to alter the pitch, the right hand strums or plucks.

Instrument challenges

Coordination, fine motor skills and finger agility in both hands. Some styles have very advanced strumming techniques for the right hand.

Starting ages

There are downsized versions of the instrument, but your child needs to understand the dangers of electricity, so around eight or nine.

Student adaptations

1/2 and 3/4 size student guitars.

Opportunities

Mainly rock and pop and some jazz.

Listening tips

Deep Purple: Smoke on the Water

Jimi Hendrix: All Along the Watchtower

Nirvana: Smells like Teen Spirit

Joe Satriani: Surfing with the Alien

The electric guitar

Star players ★ ★ ★ ★ ★ ★

★ John McLaughlin

★ Jimmy Page

★ Slash

★ Steve Vai

★ ★ ★ ★ ★ ★ ★ ★

Instrument price

From around £125 for a starter outfit including amp.

Plucked strings

The electric bass

Star players ★ ★ ★ ★ ★ ★

★ Michael 'Flea' Balzary

★ Stuart Hamm

★ Jaco Pastorius

★ Victor Wooten

★ ★ ★ ★ ★ ★ ★ ★

Instrument price
From £125 for student outfit including an amp.

Popularity
Popular.

How to play it
The left hand holds down the strings to alter the pitch, the right strums, plucks or slaps.

Instrument challenges
Coordinating left and right hands, a good sense of timekeeping and rhythm.

Starting ages
Usually around nine or ten, but student models make an earlier start possible.

Student adaptations
1/2 size bass kits.

Opportunities
Rock, pop, reggae, blues, Latin, funk and jazz bands.

Listening tips
The Beatles: Help!

Metallica: Orion

Miles Davis/Marcus Miller: Tutu

Queen: Another One Bites the Dust

Popularity

More rarely played.

How to play it

The fingertips and thumbs pluck the strings and the feet operate the pedals to alter the pitch.

Instrument challenges

Thinking ahead, good hand–eye and hand to foot coordination, good ear for intonation (tuning).

Starting ages

Possible from 5 years old, but usually around 7 or 8 years old.

Student adaptations

There are many variations of harp in different sizes with a range of string numbers. Children will usually start on a smaller folk version.

Opportunities

Symphony orchestra, chamber music, Celtic and other traditional music and many genres of pop.

Popular styles

Mainly classical for the pedal harp, folk, jazz and pop for the folk harp (sometimes also called a Celtic harp).

Star players ★ ★ ★ ★ ★

★ Yolanda Kondonassis
★ Loreena McKennitt
★ Marisa Robles
★ David Watkins

★ ★ ★ ★ ★ ★ ★ ★ ★ ★

The concert harp

(or pedal harp)

Listening tips

Edmar Castañeda: Afro Seis

George Frideric Handel: Harp Concerto in B Flat Major

Sergei Prokofiev: Prelude, Op. 12, No. 7

Pyotr Ilyich Tchaikovsky: The Nutcracker: Waltz of the Flowers

Instrument price

Expensive; a forty-seven string beginner's pedal harp is around £7,500; professional harps easily cost £20,000 and more.

The piano

Popularity

The most popular of the instruments.

How to play it

The fingers of both hands are used to press down the keys, both simultaneously and successively.

Instrument challenges

Fine motor skills, independent hand movements, reading two lines of music in different clefs at once.

Starting ages

Possible from three onwards, but it is very common to start around six or seven.

Keyboard

Popular styles

Most common styles are classical and jazz.

Student adaptations

Acoustic and digital.

Opportunities

Self-sufficient, but always needed to accompany other instruments, jazz bands, swing bands, chamber music.

Listening tips

Frédéric Chopin: Studies Op. 12 and Op. 25

Bill Evans: Time Remembered

Jerry Lee Lewis: Great Balls of Fire

Sergei Rachmaninoff: Piano Concerto No. 3

Star players ★ ★ ★ ★ ★ ★

★ Elton John

★ Svjatoslav Richter

★ Oscar Peterson

★ Mitsuko Uchida

★ ★ ★ ★ ★ ★ ★ ★ ★

Instrument price

New uprights from around £1,500 and rentals start at as little as £25 a month.

Popularity

Very popular.

How to play it

The fingers of both hands depress keys.

Instrument challenges

Fine motor skills, reading in two clefs at once, ideally computer skills to make full use of the instrument's possibilities.

Starting ages

Can be started very young, but usually around seven or eight.

Popular styles

Mainly pop, rock and jazz.

Student adaptations

None needed.

Opportunities

Many schools run keyboard groups, there are keyboard orchestras and, of course, keyboards are vital in popular music.

The electronic keyboard

Star players ★ ★ ★ ★ ★ ★

- ★ Chick Corea
- ★ Herbie Hancock
- ★ Rick Wakeman
- ★ Stevie Wonder

★ ★ ★ ★ ★ ★ ★ ★ ★

Listening tips

Booker T & The MGs: Green Onions

The Doors: Changeling

Jean Michel Jarre: Oxygène

Nine Inch Nails: The Great Collapse

Instrument price
Very affordable from around £100 to around £500.

Woodwind

What are the most common woodwind instruments?

- ◆ flute
- ◆ clarinet
- ◆ oboe
- ◆ bassoon
- ◆ recorder
- ◆ saxophone

What styles of music do woodwind instruments play?

Classical, baroque, folk, jazz and pop.

 Info point

Looking after your instrument

Regular servicing by a professional is needed to check key mechanisms are in good condition.

fllute

saxophone

clarinet

Accessories

- extra reeds (oboes, bassoons, clarinets)
- lint-free cleaning cloth (and rod for flutes) for cleaning the insides of the instrument
- fine microfibre cloth for cleaning the outside of the instrument

Did you know?

The woodwind family is very old. A flute made from the bone of a vulture was recently found in a cave in Germany and has been confirmed to be 35,000 years old.

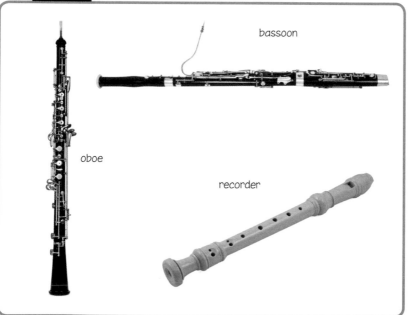

bassoon

oboe

recorder

The flute

Popularity

Very popular.

How to play it

The player blows air over an edge in the mouthpiece, and stops the tone holes to alter the pitch.

Instrument challenges

Establishing a good sound, getting used to holding the instrument, developing a good ear for intonation (tuning), breath control.

Starting ages

Around eight or nine, possibly earlier with a curved joint flute.

Student adaptations

Curved head joints, which enable smaller players to hold the flute in a comfortable way.

Opportunities

Classical orchestra, wind band, flute choirs, jazz ensembles and folk music.

Listening tips

Georges Bizet: Entr'acte from Carmen

Ian Clarke: Zoom Tube

Hamilton Harty: In Ireland

Wolfgang Amadeus Mozart: Concerto for Flute No. 2 in D Major

Woodwind

Instrument price

From £200 for curved head joint student models, to around £3,000 for high-quality advanced models.

Star players ★ ★ ★ ★ ★

★ William Bennett

★ James Galway

★ Eric Dolphy

★ Jean-Pierre Rampal

★ ★ ★ ★ ★ ★ ★ ★ ★

Popularity

Less frequently played but much in demand.

How to play it

The player blows through a reed to create the sound and the fingers shut keys covering the tone holes to alter the pitch.

Instrument challenges

Producing and controlling a sound require patience and are difficult, breath control, developing a good ear for intonation (tuning), progress can be slow.

Starting ages

Around ten or eleven, but if using a specially developed children's instrument from seven or eight.

Student adaptations

Various simplified 'junior' versions (depending on manufacturer).

Opportunities

Classical orchestra, military bands, wind bands, rarely rock, pop or jazz.

Listening tips

Ennio Morricone: Gabriel's Oboe

Wolfgang Amadeus Mozart: Concerto in C major

Francis Poulenc: Sonata for Oboe and Piano

Ralph Vaughan Williams: Oboe Concerto

The oboe

Star players ★ ★ ★ ★ ★ ★

★ Maurice Bourgue

★ Heinz Holliger

★ Albrecht Mayer

★ Hansjorg Schellenberger

★ ★ ★ ★ ★ ★ ★ ★ ★

Instrument price

From around £150 for a children's model without keys, designed for the first year of learning, to £600–£1,000 for a 'real' student oboe (with some simplification of mechanism).

35

The clarinet

Popularity

Very popular.

How to play it

The player blows through a reed and mouthpiece to create the sound, the hands shut off keys and tone holes to alter the pitch.

Instrument challenges

Dexterity (fingerings can get complicated), developing a good ear for intonation (tuning), breath control.

Starting ages

Around nine, possible earlier on the Kinder Klari.

Student adaptations

Reduced-size clarinets are available.

Opportunities

Classical orchestra, clarinet choirs, wind bands, chamber music, jazz bands and ensembles, traditional and Klezmer groups (traditional Jewish music).

Listening tips

Aaron Copland: Clarinet Concerto

The Dukes of Dixieland: Clarinet Marmalade

Gerald Finzi: Clarinet Concerto

Wolfgang Amadeus Mozart: Clarinet Quintet

Instrument price

Starting from £189 for Bflat and Kinder Klari, cheaper and more robust models made from resin.

Star players ★ ★ ★ ★ ★

★ Benny Goodman

★ Emma Johnson

★ Sabine Meyer

★ Richard Stoltzman

Woodwind

Popularity

Less frequently played but much in demand.

How to play it

The player blows through a reed to create the sound, the fingers cover the tone holes and keys.

Instrument challenges

Dexterity (fingerings on the bassoon can get complicated and involve all ten fingers, including thumbs).

Starting ages

Usually eleven to thirteen, but with a mini bassoon, seven to nine.

Student adaptations

Short reach and mini bassoon (tuned to a different base note from adult bassons).

Opportunities

Bassoon players are always in demand.

Listening tips

Paul Dukas: The Sorcerer's Apprentice, Soundtrack to Disney's Fantasia (the contrabassoon)

Edward Elgar: Romance for Bassoon and Orchestra in D Minor, Op. 62

Wolfgang Amadeus Mozart: Bassoon Concerto in B flat major

Igor Stravinsky: The Rite of Spring

The bassoon

Star players ★ ★ ★ ★ ★ ★

★ Maurice Allard

★ Sergio Azzolini

★ Bernard Garfield

★ Klaus Thunemann

★ ★ ★ ★ ★ ★ ★ ★

Instrument price

Wooden mini bassoons from around £1,000, full-size student models also starting around £1,000.

The saxophone

Popularity

Very popular.

How to play it

The player blows through a reed to create the sound and the fingers shut keys, covering the tone holes to alter the pitch.

Instrument challenges

Fine motor skills for fast fingerwork, developing a good ear for intonation (tuning), breath control.

Starting ages

Your child will need to choose a saxophone which fits their hand span and they also need to be able to support the weight of the instrument, so many players start at nine or ten years old.

Student adaptations

The Alphasax is an adapted alto saxophone with less keywork. It is less heavy than a standard alto saxophone and can be played from seven years onwards.

Opportunities

Military bands, wind bands, symphony orchestras and, of course, jazz and pop music.

Listening tips

John Coltrane: Giant Steps

Paule Maurice: Tableaux de Provence

Maceo Parker: Pass the Peas

Gerry Rafferty: Baker Street

Instrument price

Some very good Chinese models from around £250 for an alto sax, some lightweight UK models from around £400.

Star players ★ ★ ★ ★ ★ ★

★ Candy Dulfer

★ Marcel Mule

★ Charlie Parker

★ Sonny Rollins

★ ★ ★ ★ ★ ★ ★ ★ ★

Woodwind

Popularity

Very popular beginner's instrument, less often taken to a professional level, although there is now much renewed interest in Early Music.

How to play it

Air is blown into a mouthpiece and both hands cover the tone holes.

Instrument challenges

Dexterity for fast fingerwork, breath and tongue control, developing a good ear for intonation (tuning).

Starting ages

Three onwards.

Student adaptations

None required.

Opportunities

Recorder consorts, early music ensembles, traditional and folk music.

Listening tips

Arcangelo Corelli: La Follia

Hans Martin-Linde: Music for a Bird

Antonio Vivaldi: Recorder Concerto in C Major

Chen Yi: The Ancient Chinese Beauty

The recorder

Star players ★ ★ ★ ★ ★ ★

- ★ Frans Brüggen
- ★ Michala Petri
- ★ The Royal Wind Music
- ★ Maurice Steger

★ ★ ★ ★ ★ ★ ★ ★

Instrument price
£4.99–£24.99 for a beginner soprano recorder.

The brass

What are the most common brass instruments?

♦ trumpet
♦ French horn
♦ trombone
♦ tuba

What styles of music do brass instruments play?

Classical, baroque, jazz, pop, folk, reggae and ska.

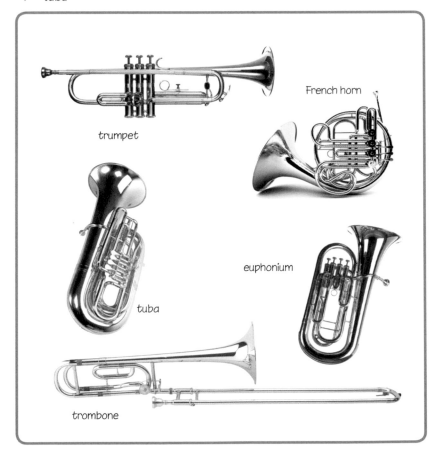

trumpet

French horn

tuba

euphonium

trombone

Did you know?

Early versions of trumpets were found in Egyptian pyramids and are thought to be 3,500 years old.

Accessories

- lubrication fluid (ask your teacher for help with lubricating valves)
- cloth for wiping moisture off the outside of the instrument
- various stops and mutes which are inserted into the bell of the instrument to muffle and alter the sound (optional)

The trumpet

Popularity

A very popular brass instrument.

How to play it

The player blows a 'raspberry' into the mouthpiece and the right hand depresses the valves to alter the pitch.

Instrument challenges

Establishing and maintaining a good embouchure (lip muscle control), developing a good ear for intonation (tuning).

Starting ages

From six onwards, but usually eight or nine.

Student adaptations

The cornet is a smaller alternative to the trumpet.

Opportunities

Vital in the classical orchestra, brass bands, brass quintets, wind bands, jazz, rock and pop, a very versatile instrument!

Popular styles

Classical, jazz and pop.

Listening tips

Aaron Copland: Quiet City

Dick Dale and The Deltones: Miserlou

Miles Davis: On Green Dolphin Street

Johann Hepomuk Hummel: Trumpet Concerto in E flat

Instrument price
Student models from around £120.

Star players ★ ★ ★ ★ ★

★ Alison Balsom

★ Dizzy Gillespie

★ Tine Thing Helseth

★ Sergei Nakariakov

★ ★ ★ ★ ★ ★ ★ ★ ★

The brass

Popularity

Less popular than some other brass instruments but very much in demand.

How to play it

The horn rests on the player's lap, the right hand is placed inside the bell for support and to alter the sound and the left hand depresses the three valves to alter the pitch.

Instrument challenges

Producing and controlling the sound (horns are temperamental and it is easy to 'mispitch' or 'fluff' a note completely).

Starting ages

Possible from seven, but usually nine to eleven.

Popular styles

Mainly classical.

Student adaptations

Single and double horns, Kinderhorns.

Opportunities

Vital in the classical orchestra, brass quintets, wind bands.

Listening tips

Wolfgang Amadeus Mozart: Horn Concerto No. 2

Camille Saint-Saëns: Concert piece for French Horn and Orchestra Op. 94

Howard Shore: Lord of the Rings soundtrack

Richard Strauss: Horn Concerto No. 2 in E Flat

The French horn

Star players ★ ★ ★ ★ ★

★ Hermann Baumann

★ Dennis Brain

★ Radek Baborak

★ John Cerminaro

Instrument price

Beginner's outfits starting around £170, but make sure you get them checked by someone knowledgeable for playability; £500 for a double horn.

The trombone

Popularity

A popular brass instrument.

How to play it

The player blows a 'raspberry' into the mouthpiece and moves a slide to alter the notes.

Instrument challenges

Developing a good ear for intonation (tuning), lip control (embouchure), stamina and breath control.

Starting ages

Usually around eight or nine.

Popular styles

Classical, jazz and pop.

Student adaptations

There are mini trombones and slide extensions for younger players and there is now also the 'pbone', a great sounding and resilient plastic trombone for around £100!

Opportunities

Classical orchestra, brass bands, brass quintets, wind bands, jazz ensembles, rock and pop, very versatile!

Listening tips

The Birdlanders: I'll Remember April

Aaron Copland: Fanfare for the Common Man

Jan Sandström: Sång Till Lotta

Richard Wagner: Ride of the Valkyries

Instrument price

Very affordable student versions from around £100, it is important to find the right mouthpiece!

Star players ★ ★ ★ ★ ★ ★

★ Ian Bousfield

★ Christian Lindberg

★ Mark Nightingale

★ Dennis Rollins

The brass

Popularity

Not very popular.

How to play it

Sitting down with the instrument on your lap and the bell facing up. The player buzzes his lips into the mouthpiece and depresses the valves to make different pitches.

Instrument challenges

Maintaining embouchure (lip control), stamina for breath control).

Popular styles

Classical and jazz (in particular, Dixie and trad).

Starting ages

Around 7 years old for the euphonium or baritone and around 11 or 12 years old for the tuba (this is very much dependent on size and stamina).

Student adaptations

Many beginners start on the smaller baritone or euphonium and progress to the tuba.

Opportunities

Orchestras, military and wind bands, jazz.

Star players ★ ★ ★ ★ ★ ★

- ★ Øystein Baadsvik
- ★ Alan Baer
- ★ John Fletcher
- ★ James Gourlay

★ ★ ★ ★ ★ ★ ★ ★ ★

The tuba

Listening tips

Dirty Dozen Band: Ain't Nothing But a Party

Edward Gregson: Tuba Concerto

Joseph Horovitz: Euphonium Concerto

Modest Mussorgsky: Night on Bald Mountain

Instrument price

Around £1,000 for a compact beginner's tuba.

Percussion

Percussion

What are the percussion instruments?

The percussion family has the largest number of members of all the instrument families and they come in a bewildering variety of shapes and sizes from the tiny high-sounding triangle to the large and thunderous bass drum. The biggest difference between percussion instruments is that some instruments are tuned (they produce higher and lower sounds) and others are untuned. The drum kit is an example of an untuned instrument, whereas the timpani are tuned.

What styles of music do percussion instruments play?

Rock and pop, jazz, classical music, folk, traditional music from around the world, e.g. samba and taiko.

 Info point

Looking after your ears!

Many percussion instruments are very loud (including the drum kit) so it is important to protect your hearing when playing and practising a percussion instrument.

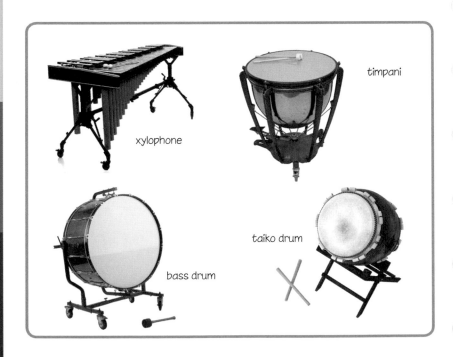

xylophone

timpani

bass drum

taiko drum

 Info point

Buy, borrow or rent?

Many orchestral percussion instruments are very expensive. Aspiring timpanists and orchestral percussionists usually come to an arrangement with their school or music teacher.

Accessories

- mallets and drumsticks
- foot pedals

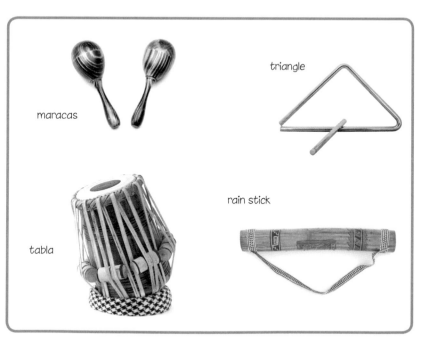

maracas

triangle

tabla

rain stick

The drum kit

Popularity

Very popular.

How to play it

The player uses sticks and foot pedals to hit the various drums.

Instrument challenges

Independent movement of arms and legs, good coordination, sense of rhythm and timekeeping, stamina. Protect your ears during practice sessions!

Starting ages

Possible from six but usually from eight or nine.

Student adaptations

1/2 size junior drum kits are available; electric drum kits allow the player to practise with headphones.

Opportunities

Very wid-ranging covering all the genres, but most important in jazz, rock and pop.

Listening tips

Billy Cobham: Spectrum

Metallica: Master of Puppets

Paul Simon: Fifty Ways to Leave your Lover

Tower of Power: Soul with a Capital S

Instrument price

From around £160 for student kits. Electronic drum kits tend to be more expensive, starting around £400.

Star players ★ ★ ★ ★ ★

★   Carter Beauford

★   Vinnie Colaiuta

★   Keith Moon

★   Tony Williams

★ ★ ★ ★ ★ ★ ★ ★

Popularity

Popular.

How to play it

Hit, shake, scrape, rub or any other action that sets the instrument into vibration!

Instrument challenges

Good coordination, a sense of time and rhythm; timpanists also need to develop a good ear for intonation (tuning).

Starting ages

Six onwards. Depends on the method, instrument and teacher chosen. Beginners often start on the drum kit or snare drums and sometimes xylophone.

Student adaptations

Half-size drum kits, snare drums, xylophones with varying numbers of bars.

Opportunities

Orchestras, samba bands, military bands, taiko groups, steel bands, African drumming groups

Percussion

Star players ★ ★ ★ ★ ★ ★

★ Christopher Lamb

★ Evelyn Glennie

★ Colin Currie

★ Talvin Singh

★ ★ ★ ★ ★ ★ ★ ★ ★

Listening tips

Tito Puento: Ran Kan Kan

Gocoo: Zyu-zing

Camille Saint-Saëns: Carnival of the Animals (Fossils movement) and Danse Macabre

Nitin Sawhney: The Conference

Instrument price

Snare drum plus stand £100, three-octave rosewood xylophone £150.

The voice

The voice

Listening tips

Gregorio Allegri: Miserere

Leonard Bernstein: West Side Story (Broadway Production)

Eduardo di Capua: O Sole Mio (The Three Tenors)

Amy Winehouse: Back to Black

Instrument price Free!

Popularity

Extremely popular.

How to play it

The vocal cords vibrate on the out-breath and create soundwaves.

Popular styles

From pop to classical, jazz to metal!

Student adaptations

Children have a limited range of notes they can sing comfortably and it is important for young voices to sing the right repertoire. Even adults can easily damage their voice through unsuitable repertoire or overuse.

Opportunities

Choirs, vocal ensembles, pop and rock bands, opera, musicals.

Star players ★ ★ ★ ★ ★ ★

- ★ Jon Bon Jovi
- ★ Maria Callas
- ★ Ella Fitzgerald
- ★ Nat King Cole

★ ★ ★ ★ ★ ★ ★ ★ ★

Traditional instruments

Accordion

The accordion was first invented in Germany around the early nineteenth century. It comes in two versions: the piano and button accordion. One has keys (like a piano) and the other has only buttons to produce different pitches. The sound is created by internal bellows, which force air through reeds inside the instrument, similar to the reeds of a harmonica.

Popularity

Very popular in traditional music of many cultures.

Instrument price

From around £250 for a beginner's instrument to around £500 for an instrument with the full range.

Ukulele

The ukulele looks very much like a guitar and was developed in Hawaii in the nineteenth century. A standard soprano ukulele measures only 53 cm from top to bottom, making it a very popular instrument for children. It is played very much like a guitar, with the left hand holding down the strings and the right hand plucking or strumming the four strings.

Popularity

Becoming quite popular again!

Instrument price

Very affordable from around £30. Make sure the ukulele has geared tuning pegs.

Other traditional instruments include:

Bagpipes, steel pans, Gaelic harp, mandolin, harmonica, African and Latin percussion, penny whistle, didgeridoo, sitar, tabla, Chinese and Japanese flutes; the list is endless.

Finding a teacher

Finding the right teacher for your child is one of the most important aspects to consider in their musical development. It is a very individual choice too and what suits one child might not necessarily suit another. This chapter looks at some of the key qualities that make a good teacher and gives advice on where to start your search. It also covers helpful questions to ask yourself, your child and the prospective teacher, so that you can find the best fit for your child.

What makes a good teacher?

Cast your mind back to school. We all knew who the best teachers were, and we also knew which ones weren't so good! Putting a finger on what exactly makes a good teacher is a bit trickier. Here are some of the qualities that make a good teacher. The list below is by no means exhaustive and it is also geared towards a beginner's needs.

Communication skills: Mastering your subject and being able to explain it to another person, particularly a beginner, are two very different things. A good teacher can do both and uses a wide variety of methods such as games, analogies and stories to explain posture, technique and musical concepts in the simplest way possible. A good teacher enjoys communicating and listens carefully to their student.

Fair and flexible: A good teacher wants to help each of their pupils to achieve their full potential, regardless of their ability level. They have different expectations for their students and don't compare them to one another. They also recognise that students learn in different ways and they are able to adapt their teaching to each child's changing needs.

Creating playing opportunities outside music lessons: Making music with others is vital to maintaining your child's interest in playing, developing their skills and performing. A good teacher will encourage your child to engage in opportunities outside lessons such as local ensembles, choirs and holiday courses, playing in local festivals, competitions and informal performances.

Role model: An inspiring teacher that your child looks up to and wants to emulate plays a vital part in your child's enjoyment of, and success with, learning an instrument. Although a good mastery of their instrument is necessary, your child's first teacher does not need to be a virtuoso player. Younger beginners in particular tend to respond best to warmth, encouragement and support. A smattering of humour is usually also appreciated.

Enthusiasm and generosity: The ability to enthuse and inspire is crucial, especially when teaching beginners. Inspirational teachers have a deep love of their subject and a generosity of spirit to share this enthusiasm.

Sensitivity: Beginners benefit from a relaxed and encouraging atmosphere, where it is safe to make mistakes and they are not pushed too hard. Of course, good teachers will encourage their pupils to practise regularly, but they will also encourage them to have plenty of fun in a supportive environment.

Different learning styles

We all have our own unique way of processing and learning new information and it has long been recognised that one approach does not fit all. A good teacher will identify your child's preferred learning styles and tap into them. Here are the main types of learning style:

V	**visual:** prefers to learn through looking at graphic representations of ideas.
A	**auditory:** prefers to learn through listening to instructions, learning by rote, talking things through to understand concepts better.
K	**kinaesthetic:** prefers to learn by doing a physical activity and uses 'finger memory' to remember patterns in the music.
C	**combination learning:** prefers to draw on two or more of the above learning styles. Most people use more than one learning style.

How a teacher would explain a bowing pattern on the violin using different learning methods:

Type of learner	Teaching method
Visual	Demonstrating the bowing pattern or drawing a diagram of the pattern
Auditory	Giving verbal instructions
Kinaesthetic	Encouraging the student to try out the movement. The teacher modifies the bow position and movement gently when necessary.

The learning curve

Quite often learners reach a plateau and then suddenly jump ahead. This is also a question of learning styles: your child might be a sequential learner, who builds each new step on the previous one, or your child could be a learner who needs to absorb many different aspects of what's taught simultaneously, before they suddenly get it.

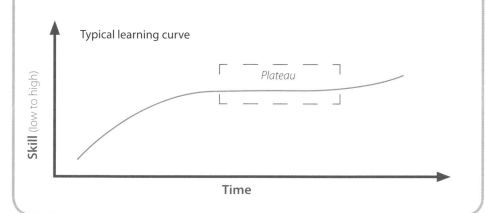

Typical learning curve

Skill (low to high)

Plateau

Time

Where to look for a teacher

It is worth taking plenty of time over choosing the right teacher for your child as music tuition is a long-term commitment and a good teacher–pupil relationship is very important.

There are three options for you to arrange for music lessons for your child:

- through the local music service/hub

- a peripatetic teacher at your child's school

- a private music teacher offering lessons at their house.

The principles of good teaching do not change from one setting to another, but the amount of choice you will have over the teacher, instrument and lesson style may vary.

Music hubs

What are music hubs?

In September 2012 music education hubs took over the responsibility of music provision for children aged between five and eighteen years from the local authority-run music services in England. This was a result of the recommendations set out in Darren Henley's review of music education and the subsequent National Music Plan.

What do music services/hubs offer?

What is offered by music services/hubs will differ around the country. However, every music service/hub aims to offer the following services that were outlined in the National Plan for Music Education[7]:

- ensure that every child aged 5–18 has the opportunity to learn a musical instrument (other than voice) through whole-class ensemble teaching programmes for ideally a year (but for a minimum of a term) of weekly tuition on the same instrument

- provide opportunities to play in ensembles and to perform from an early stage

- ensure that clear progression routes are available and affordable to all young people

- develop a singing strategy to ensure that every pupil sings regularly and that choirs and other vocal ensembles are available in the area.

> *Locating your local music service/hub*
>
> Information about music services/hubs can be accessed through a database on the Federation of Music Services website **www.thefms.org** and on the Arts Council website **www.artscouncil.org.uk**

[7] *The Importance of Music: A National Plan for Music Education,* Department for Education, p 11

Individual or group instrumental lessons at school

Music services/hubs provide peripatetic teachers for local state schools and coordinate workshops and ensembles across their geographical area. Independent schools usually organise their own peripatetic teaching, but may in some cases choose to work with music services/hubs. Peripatetic teachers at schools should have been CRB checked and are normally well qualified, although qualifications can vary considerably.

Things to be aware of when choosing music lessons at your child's school

Advantages:

1. Your child will be learning in a safe and familiar environment during school hours when they are the most alert.

2. It is a relatively stress-free option for both you and your child as you don't need to ferry them to and from lessons after school.

3. If your child is learning in a group with their friends this can be a really fun way to start learning an instrument and good experience of playing with and listening to other young musicians.

Possible drawbacks:

1. Your child may not be able to get lessons on some of the more unusual instruments.

2. It may also be more difficult for you to have a say in the choice of teacher.

3. Contact with your child's teacher may also be limited with most communication taking place through the weekly practice booklet.

Missing class lessons

Your child will usually need to miss part of their normal classroom lessons to attend instrumental tuition. Most schools operate a rotation system for music lessons so that your child does not always miss the same subject.

Lessons with a private music teacher

Evidently, if you employ a private teacher you have most control over the choice of teacher and lesson style. Finding a good teacher may take quite a lot of time-consuming research at the start but it is definitely worth the effort.

How to find a private music teacher

- Friends' recommendations: this can be an excellent way of finding a suitable teacher in your area but be aware that what works well for your friend's child is not guaranteed to work for yours.

- Music hub recommendations.

- Adverts in the local press or on **www.gumtree.com**.

- Contact music teachers' associations such as the European Piano Teachers Association, the Federation of Music Services or the Musicians' Union (see useful resources for more information).

- Online databases of approved teachers run by the ISM (Incorporated Society of Musicians) **www.ism.org** and the MU (Musicians' Union) **www.musicteachers.co.uk**.

- For-profit tutor websites, where teachers can post their profile, e.g. **http://www.musicteachers.co.uk**.

- Teachers' personal websites and blogs.

- Local festivals or concerts where other children might be performing.

Private lessons at home or the teacher's studio?

Some teachers are able to visit your house to give lessons. If you are considering having private lessons at home, you will need a suitably sized room that is free from disturbances such as television and siblings. Teachers usually charge more to come to you so make sure that you enquire about this and are happy to pay the extra cost. It is possible that your child may miss out on resources, a good acoustic and additional activities that may be available at the teacher's house.

Common questions

How much do lessons cost?

Whole-class instrumental lessons organised by the local music service/hub are free for the child in the first instance and there are schemes available to help pupils who may not be able to pay for musical opportunities after this stage. The ISM (Incorporated Society of Musicians) frequently runs a survey of fees charged by music teachers and the results are freely accessible on their website. On most tutor search sites, teachers will give an indication of the fees they charge as well as other useful details such as whether they offer other services such as extra music theory or aural lessons. Bear in mind that at this stage in particular the chemistry between your child and their teacher is one of the most important criteria, so an expensive teacher might not necessarily be the best choice for your child.

What qualifications should I look out for?

When it comes to music qualifications, it is important to remember that some of the best teachers have no formal qualifications of any sort. The success of a teacher's students and word of mouth from other parents will be a reliable indicator of a teacher's qualities.

Most music college and conservatoire courses include modules on instrumental teaching and also are excellent indicators of musical knowledge and achievement. The content of university music courses can be more diverse, so it is a good idea to ask the teacher whether they have an additional teaching qualification, or whether teaching was part of their course. Diplomas from external boards such as ABRSM and Trinity Guildhall are also good qualifications.

Info point

Discounted music tuition

One of the aims of the music services/hubs is to ensure access for all by giving discounts and reduced fees to financially disadvantaged students. The chances are that if your child is eligible for free school meals they should also be eligible for discounted music tuition. Ask your child's school or local music service/hub for more details.

How long do lessons last?

Lesson duration can be very variable. If your child has lessons at school or the local music service/hub, it will depend on their policy. The table below indicates what might be desirable, but depending on your child's development and the setting of their lessons, shorter durations might be indicated.

Age and ability	Average length of lesson
Young beginners (*3–7 years old*)	15–30 mins
Older beginners	30–45 mins

How often should my child have lessons?

Most children who learn an instrument at school or at a music service/hub will have a lesson once a week during term time. If your child learns with a private teacher there may be the option of having lessons during the school holidays too.

Individual or group instrumental lessons?

You may be offered a choice between individual lessons or group lessons.

Both styles of learning offer many benefits and some drawbacks so it is worth being aware of these before making a decision with your child.

Info point

Certain instruments are more likely to be taught in group lessons, e.g. recorder or violin, whereas other instruments such as the piano tend to be taught more frequently in one-to-one lessons.

Advantages and disadvantages of group learning:

Advantages:

★ Often more informal than one-to-one lessons.

★ Students can learn from their peers.

★ Plenty of opportunities to play in a group with other learners.

★ Can be cheaper, so a good way of trying out an instrument before committing to individual lessons.

★ Children can be motivated to practice and improve by their peers.

Disadvantages:

★ Children progress at different rates. Experienced teachers will be able to compensate to some extent, but if attainment diverges too much it can become frustrating for both advancing and lagging students.

★ In the case of mixed instrumental learning, the teacher will not necessarily be a specialist in all the instruments, so some children will receive expert tuition, while others will not. This might be a problem for more advanced students.

★ More advanced learners (beyond Grades 4–5) may benefit from individual tuition in addition to group learning.

Should I attend lessons?

Most teachers welcome parents to sit in on lessons regularly when a child has first started lessons. Some teaching methods actually require the attendance of an adult (Suzuki). If your child is having lessons at school or at your local music hub, attending lessons may not be possible for you but it always worth enquiring if it might be possible on an occasional basis, or when there are problems with progress.

If you have chosen a private teacher, for safety reasons it is always a good idea to sit in on the first few lessons (see the section on Safety on p63) and also to check that you are happy with your choice of teacher. You will also be very well informed about the work your child needs to do outside lessons.

In the long-term it's worth bearing in mind that sitting in on lessons can be very distracting for both your child and their teacher. Also, in order for your child to become an independent learner, they will eventually need to attend lessons on their own and translate what they've learnt in a lesson into practice at home.

Consultation/trial lessons

Requesting a consultation lesson

If you are considering lessons with a private teacher, try to arrange a consultation lesson before committing. This will enable you to (within limits) see whether the chemistry between your child and the teacher is right and to ask any questions you may have. Some schools and music services/hubs prefer children to commit for at least a term to see if instrument and teacher are a good fit instead of having a trial lesson.

How to approach a teacher

Before going to the consultation lesson it is worth thinking about some of the things that matter to you and to your child, for example if your child is particularly interested in a certain genre, e.g. rock and pop. Be tactful in the way that you ask questions: you don't want to give your prospective teacher the impression that you are 'interrogating' them.

Here are some suggested questions to get started with:

- ☐ Which days and hours do you teach?

- ☐ How long would a trial lesson cost and how long would it last?

- ☐ Do you teach very young beginners if that applies to your child?

- ☐ Explain that your child is particularly interested in a certain genre of music. Are you happy teaching this genre?

- ☐ Can I sit in on the trial lesson? (The answer to this question should always be 'yes'.)

Questions from a prospective teacher

A teacher may also have some initial questions for you, such as:

- ☐ your child's age

- ☐ your child's musical experience, e.g. are they a complete beginner? can they read music?

- ☐ their preferred genre of music

- ☐ your child's temperament

- ☐ your expectations and your child's expectations

Questions to ask at a trial lesson

When asking questions at a trial lesson, it is important to make it clear to the potential teacher why you are asking. Mention that you are concerned for a good fit between teacher and student, and emphasise that you are not trying to judge the teacher. Rather than asking questions directly, it is probably a good idea to put them into a personal context relevant to your situation. For example, the question regarding practice could be couched as 'David is really still very playful and he finds it hard to sit down to do his homework. What are your expectations for the amount of practice needed and do you have any advice for me?'

Here are some ideas that could be used as a starting point for discussion at an appropriate point during a trial lesson:

? Can I sit in on a few lessons at the beginning? (The answer to this question should always be 'yes'.)

? What are your expectations with regard to practice?

? What is your attitude to exams?

? Do you teach theory and musicianship?

? What are your expectations from a prospective pupil?

? Could you advise me on buying an instrument for my child?

Info point

Professional development

It is easy for private music teachers in particular to become isolated and out of touch with developments in the teaching profession. It is best not to ask a teacher directly about professional development but a teacher might mention that they have been taking CPD courses or have attended an exam board conference. This is a definite plus point as it shows that they are keeping abreast of current best practice.

Info point

Asking for clarification

Don't be afraid to ask for clarification if you do not understand something the teacher says. If you are having trouble understanding the teacher's explanations, the chances are that your child might have similar problems.

What happens in a music lesson?

A lesson will usually cover a variety of aspects of music making from playing to listening and music theory. In the first few lessons, the teacher will probably spend time getting to know your child, introducing them to their new instrument and explaining how to look after it. They may also do some general musicianship activities for several weeks such as clapping rhythms or singing before picking up the instrument and playing simple pieces. Each teacher does things differently. The main thing at this stage is that your child is enjoying the lessons and learning about music.

A good teacher will cover the following elements, although not necessarily in every lesson:

✓ Looking after the instrument (e.g. putting the instrument together and back in its case, cleaning it)

✓ Learning to tune the instrument

✓ Warm-ups (exercises to ease your child into playing at the beginning of a session and reduce the risk of injury)

✓ Technique (the nuts and bolts of playing – e.g. playing a scale or a run on the piano, or how to use the pedal properly)

✓ Playing repertoire (the pieces your child is playing)

✓ Aural awareness (e.g. identifying the basic elements of music such as intervals – the distance between notes, melodies and rhythms)

✓ Music theory (the study of how music works, for example learning about music from different periods and identifying key elements of the building blocks of music such as rhythm)

✓ Musicianship (playing from memory, sight-reading, improvising).

How can I make sure my child is safe?

There is currently a big debate on the issue of child protection in relation to music lessons. Teachers are often in a situation where they are in close proximity to pupils and often in one-to-one situations. They may need to adjust posture, demonstrate a good hand position or diaphragm movement.

There are currently no requirements for private music tutors to be police checked, although many undergo voluntary disclosure anyway and should be aware of child protection

issues. Most organisations such as schools or music hubs will require their staff to undergo mandatory enhanced Criminal Records Bureau (CRB) checks and child protection training but it is worth double-checking, if you are concerned.

You should talk about physical contact with your child's instrumental teacher and come to an agreement about touching as a means of adjusting posture and technique depending on how you feel about this thorny issue.

Opinion is divided on this issue and many forthright dicsussions have been led on the subject (see The debate, below).

The debate

Communicating with your child's teacher

Good communicaton between you, your child and your child's teacher is a really important factor when it comes to your child's enjoyment of and success in music making. Depending on where and with whom your child has their music lessons you will have varying degree of contact with your child's teacher.

Many parents can feel a bit intimidated when talking to a music teacher, in particular if they consider themselves 'unmusical'. Don't let this put you off establishing good communications with your child's music teacher. Of course, you need to strike a good balance, so as not to come across as 'aggressive' or 'pushy', but if you have concerns or worries about your child's lessons, their progress or their attitude, you need to raise these with your child's teacher. Most teachers welcome constructive parental involvement.

When to talk to your child's teacher

If your child has lessons at school you may only meet the teacher at school events, so the main form of communication will most probably be through your child's practice book. It is important that the teacher writes clear instructions in your child's practice book that both you and your child can follow together.

If your child has private lessons there will usually be a few moments to discuss issues if you drop off or collect your child. If a longer conversation is needed you might want to consider using some of the allocated lesson time to raise any issues, but be aware that you need to be discreet and that there are aspects you might not like to discuss with your child present. It might be easier to tackle whatever problem you are encountering initially via email or a telephone call.

Most teachers have busy schedules, so it is important that you can determine a time when your child's teacher can talk and is not constrained by another student arriving.

At the beginning I felt very intimidated about speaking to a teacher. I don't even know what a scale is, so I felt I could not initiate a conversation. It turned out that my fears were really unfounded, as the teacher was very approachable and friendly.

Richard

Training for exceptionally talented young musicians

Centres for Advanced Training

The Centres for Advanced Training (CATS) are organisations or consortia of organisations/partners that include existing Saturday provision at junior departments of music conservatoires and new weekend schools, after-school hours and holiday courses for exceptional young musicians aged 8–16 and dancers aged 11–16. They ensure that talented and dedicated children have appropriate, tailor-made, specialist provision even if they do not attend specialist schools. A list of the Centres for Advanced Training and information about grants can be found on the Department for Education website.

Junior conservatoire departments

All the national conservatoires run so-called junior departments, generally for 8–18-year-olds. The junior departments usually meet on Saturdays and there is often a wide range of ensembles on offer. Entrance into these departments is highly selective and usually by audition.

Open days

Junior departments run open days where parents and their children are welcome to look around the department, attend rehearsals, observe lessons (usually only if arranged in advance), talk to current students and listen to any of the concerts, workshops or masterclasses. It is often possible to arrange an appointment in advance to speak to the Heads of Department about opportunities available at the junior conservatoire.

Conservatoire programmes for young learners

Some conservatoires also run programmes for very young learners (three or four years upwards), which are non-selective but operate on a first-come, first-served basis. Be aware that these programmes are extremely popular and make sure that you sign up early (a year in advance at least) if you are interested.

A percussion lesson at Junior Guildhall.
Photo © Richard Olivier

Practising

Practising at home is the first step along the path to becoming an independent musician. A good teacher will play an important part in showing your child how to practise and will also inspire them to do so. Most children also need extra support at home from a parent or guardian in order to learn to practise regularly and effectively. Praise and encouragement also go a long way to make sure that your child enjoys practising. Fortunately, there are many ways in which you can support your child and you don't need to be musical to help them. There are also a few things that you should avoid doing that, if left unchecked, may inhibit your child's learning rather than encourage it.

Learning an instrument isn't easy!

When you're listening to your child learning to play their first notes you may, on some occasions, secretly regret that you encouraged them to start playing an instrument in the first place! Remember that learning to play an instrument is a hugely complex undertaking and involves multitasking at a very high level!

Here are some of the new skills that your child will be learning during their lessons and will need to repeat at home:

- holding the instrument and their body in often unfamiliar positions
- using muscle groups which need to be strengthened
- making a sound and controlling it
- listening to the sound they are making and modifying it if necessary
- learning and applying music notation
- learning and understanding unfamiliar terminology
- listening to and then remembering the teacher's instructions (usually with the help of a practice book) and trying to modify their playing accordingly.

> This is a lot to take in, especially for a young child. As a result, progress may seem slow at the beginning but with a lot of patience, time and, of course, plenty of practice, things will improve.

Preparing for home practice in the lesson

During lesson time, your child's teacher will show your child:

- *how* to practise
- *what* to practise
- *how long* to practise each element.

These instructions are often written down in a practice book so that you and your child have clear instructions on what to practise at home. There is often a section for parents' comments or feedback and you may need to sign the practice book to show that your child has practised. Some teachers may encourage your child to record parts of the lesson on their mobile phone or another recording device so that they can play the lesson back at home to jog their memory. Other teachers prefer to speak to you at the end of a lesson, to phone you or use regular reports instead.

How often should practice happen and how long for?

It is much better to practise little and often rather than to try to cram everything into one massive session. Most children cannot concentrate for very long periods of time so it is best for them to practise for ten to twenty minutes on at least four or five days a week when they start playing. Developing players will need longer: around thirty to forty minutes.

Younger and even some older children do not always remember to practise, so a gentle nudge to remind your child will usually be required.

What should my child practise?

A good teacher will explain to your child during their lesson what they would like them to practise at home in preparation for the next lesson. This could include: warm-up exercises, technical exercises, repertoire, theory and listening activities.

Common questions about practice

Where is the best place to practise?

Your child's practice space should be inviting and as free as possible from distractions such as other siblings, television, or computer games. If your child is learning the piano it important to think carefully about where you are going to position the instrument as it will be difficult to move it once it has been installed.

When is the best time to practise?

Practising requires a lot of concentration and patience so your child should be mentally alert and not too tired. Practising before school can work well, as most children are quite alert in the morning and have not had a tiring school day behind them, with the added pressures of homework etc. Obviously not everyone is 'good' in the morning, so do experiment until you find a solution that suits you and your child. Most children respond well to a routine, so once you have found a suitable time, do try to adhere to it with regularity.

How should my child practise?

The teacher's instructions will often include advice on what order to practise each element. For example, warm-ups should be done before technical exercises to protect your child from over-straining too early in their practice so it is important that you stick to the order if one has been given. Your child's teacher should also indicate roughly how long your child should spend on each exercise.

Your child's teacher may also suggest different ways to approach practice that can make it both a more enjoyable and a more effective activity. The best practice sessions are both concentrated and creative. Here are a few simple variations that your child's teacher may suggest to make practising more interesting:

→ Play the piece very loudly.

→ Play it very quietly.

→ Play the piece more slowly.

→ Try to play the piece from memory.

→ Play it with your eyes closed.

→ Make up a story about the music.

→ Draw a picture to go with the piece.

Useful accessories for home practice

Some basic accessories are essential for home practice.

A solid music stand: this is essential (unless your child plays the piano or keyboard, in which case the music stand will be built into the instrument).

A full-length mirror: useful, though not essential, so that your child can check and adjust their posture and playing movements.

A metronome: useful for setting the correct tempo (i.e. the speed at which the piece needs to be played) and for encouraging steady playing. It can also be used as a very constructive practice device and is very useful for breaking material down into small chunks and repeating those chunks at varying (increasing) speeds.

Technology and other resources for practice

Recordings can be a useful way of your child getting to know and being reminded of what their pieces should sound like. Some teachers are happy to provide a CD with a recording of the piece or can suggest where you can get hold of one. If the piece is on an exam repertoire list you can often buy an edition of the sheet music with an accompanying CD that has backing tracks to play along to at home and performance tracks. The amount of additional resource material can be bewildering but your child's teacher will be able to advise on what to buy.

Your child may find that recording both their lesson (or parts of the lesson) and their playing can be very useful. It means they can always revisit something said in the lesson and it will help them to assess whether what they are playing is correct, or in tune, and what they had intended! Nearly all mobile phones now offer very high-quality recording at low prices.

How can I get involved?

This is a tricky question and depends on both your child's temperament and your child's teacher. Most teachers will welcome parental involvement with very young learners, some positively require it, like the Suzuki method.

Here are some ways in which you can get involved with practice but at the same time encourage independent learning:

Communicating with your child's teacher:

- Complete any practice record sheets that are given to you by your child's teacher.

- If there is time, ask your child's teacher at the next lesson if you and your child don't understand the practice book instructions or if your child is struggling with practice.

Helping your child to be organised:

- Make sure your child knows when their lesson is, especially if they are on a rota at school.

- Some children may benefit from having a practice calendar that you can use to encourage them to check when their next practice session is.

- Ask your child what they did in their lessons and what they're expected to achieve by the next lesson. Read over the practice book with them at the beginning of the practice session and make sure that they understand what they need to do.

- Check the practice book (or equivalent) to see whether their teacher has asked you to buy any music for a future lesson.

Being supportive and available:

- Be 'available' if they need any help during their practice or for any impromptu performances.

- Encourage them by giving positive comments on their practice (this doesn't need to be a detailed critique).

- As your child progresses, discuss with them what they like about their pieces and the composers.

Motivation

> *I like playing the violin because when I play it I have fun and I get proud.*
>
> Eric, year 5 primary pupil

Intrinsic motivation (motivation that comes from within)

Having an experienced and inspiring teacher is an extremely important part of motivating a child to practise and improve. However, most of the hard work ultimately needs to come from your child so they need to be motivated to practise and perfect their instrumental skills. In the early years you can help your child by explaining why they need to practise, and by giving them incentives to practise such as a can-do chart and by giving plenty of praise. As time goes on, many children need less parental encouragement as making music becomes its own reward and motivation!

Ideas for motivating your child

A useful analogy with sport

It helps to explain to your child why they need to practise so that they see it as a useful activity rather than a chore. One useful analogy is with training for a sport. In football training, for example, your child will not only play matches, but the coach will work separately and repetitively on fitness and skills, which are necessary to develop the game further. Just as the footballer needs to work on his skills and fitness, so a budding musician has to do the same, by practising!

The virtuous circle

I am good at something.

I improve further.

I do things I am good at more frequently, because I enjoy them.

> *Playing in cello group is great. I really like the pieces we play and seeing what the others do has helped me to read bass clef properly!*
>
> Max, age 9

Other ways to help to motivate your child

✓ Taking an interest in practice

Where appropriate, ask your child questions about what they are doing in their lessons and practice sessions. Ask for the occasional 'performance' of your child's piece.

✓ Reminding your child to practise

Remind your child about practice in a warm and encouraging way if they have forgotten or have got distracted by something else. Some children may benefit from a practice chart. Talk about playing rather than 'doing practice' as this will sound more appealing.

✓ Give postive feedback

Remember to give plenty of warm praise and encouragement, especially when your child feels that the practice has not gone well.

✓ Encourage creativity

Suggest to your child that they make up a tune using the notes that they've learnt in their lessons. This will boost their confidence and enjoyment of playing.

✓ Small rewards

Rewarding effort and concentration is an important part of motivation. Rewards don't need to be big or expensive. Good examples are: being included in the next concert, a gold sticker, can-do charts, a badge etc.

✓ Pleasing the teacher

If your child's teacher is a good role model the child will look up to them and want to impress them by showing they have improved their playing.

✓ The right repertoire

Try to work with your child's teacher to make sure the child is playing pieces that they enjoy. A well-chosen and much-loved piece can be the most effective way to boost motivation!

I carried on playing the violin, because when I see challenging music I want to be able to play it or at least try it!

Gozde, year 6 primary school pupil

Things to avoid doing

- Being overly demanding and insensitive.
- Making negative comments or pulling faces.
- Forcing your child to practise, using practice as a punishment or making your child practise when they are tired or ill.
- Putting your child under pressure if they have got something wrong.
- Parents sometimes fall accidentally into 'teacher mode' when helping their children. This can cause confusion for the child as the parent may contradict the teacher's instructions without realising it and should be avoided at all costs.

Ensemble playing

Music is first and foremost a social activity and there are many opportunities for players of any level to get involved. Playing in an ensemble is a vital part of being a musician and can make a real difference to your child's enjoyment of music and the likelihood of them becoming a successful musician.

The benefits of ensemble playing:

- ✓ Improving skills such as listening, team work and technique in a fun environment.
- ✓ Meeting like-minded children.
- ✓ Confidence is boosted.
- ✓ Motivational: playing repertoire with peers is a strong incentive to improve musical competence in both reading and playing.
- ✓ There are often chances to tour with an ensemble and to travel around the UK and to other countries.

I hadn't been out of the UK since this music tour. Being in the touring choir has been brilliant. I got to perform abroad and make new friends. It took me away from all the stuff going on at home – loved it.

Aaleyah, age 13

Children and young people making music together in Tower Hamlets (photo courtesy of Tower Hamlets Arts and Music Education Service (THAMES). Photographer: Hayley Cook (THAMES)

Types of ensembles

Schools, music services/hubs and charities run youth ensembles for a range of skill levels, from beginners to advanced students and it is never too early to get started.

Here is a list of some of the ensembles that may be on offer in your area:

- choirs
- **drumming groups** (taiko, samba, steel bands etc.)
- **folk groups**
- **world music groups**
- **jazz ensembles**
- **rock/pop bands**
- **urban music groups**
- **string ensembles, brass ensembles, woodwind ensembles, recorder ensembles, guitar ensembles, flute choirs, clarinet choirs, percussion ensembles**

- **wind bands, concert bands, symphonic bands, big bands**
- **chamber orchestras** (smaller orchestras) and symphony orchestras (larger orchestras)
- **chamber music** (various combinations of instruments – this is often only for more advanced players)
- **piano ensembles** (piano duets, trios, quartets)
- **musical theatre groups**

Junior ensembles

Children start in a junior ensemble and are given plenty of opportunities to perform in public in local school halls or concert halls. Children wishing to join the junior ensembles do not usually have to audition but may need to have at least six months of tuition.

Senior ensembles

Many of these musicians will then progress to more senior ensembles as they become more experienced and skilled. These ensembles may require an audition to allow those managing the ensembles to distribute parts that are suitable for the children. The most experienced and skilled players from the area are hand-picked, often through audition, for groups such as chamber music ensembles and the chamber orchestra or symphony orchestra who may perform in local concert halls and compete in regional and national competitions and festivals such as Music for Youth.

Going to the Tower Hamlets Saturday Music Centre is great. It has helped me develop my music and given me the opportunity of working with children of different ages and professional musicians. The Music Service also introduced me to an endangered instrument, the Bassoon. Playing the Bassoon has given me great joy and the opportunity of working with players at the LSO has been amazing

Bevlyn Anyaoku-Clough, age 12

National Youth Music Organisations (NYMOs)

The most talented musicians from the United Kingdom are selected by audition to play for National Youth Music Organisations. National Youth Music Organisations are financed in a variety of ways, including contributions from Arts Council England, the Music and Dance Scheme at the Department for Education (DfE), Youth Music, and donations from a huge number of private individuals, charitable trusts and foundations and businesses.

Talented young people from across England and beyond are brought together through a varied programme of residential rehearsal periods, weekend workshops, concerts and outreach activities. As well as providing inspirational advanced ensemble training, NYMOs offer young people the opportunity to become confident, passionate advocates who are able to lead, to help and inspire others, and to fulfil their potential as great musical role models. They perform a wide range of musical genres from Western classical to contemporary jazz and musical theatre. There is also the opportunity to perform in prestigious venues such as the Royal Albert Hall, the Bridgewater Hall (Manchester) and The Sage, Gateshead.

Entry requirements

Entry to national ensembles is via audition and applicants must be at Grade 8 standard, though it is not necessary to have taken any examinations. While the standards are very high, auditions are no longer the daunting prospect they might have been in the past, and all NYMOs aim to make their audition process a positive experience, regardless of the outcome.

I've been going to Haringey Music Centre since I was nine and I've been in loads of groups. The teachers are really good and I've been on loads of trips. I really enjoy the sessions and I'd have nothing to do outside school if it wasn't for the Music Centre.

Kate, age 15

Holiday courses

Holiday courses are a great way to keep your young musician busy during their school breaks and propel their playing to a new level through ensemble playing. They also present a good opportunity for your child to meet like-minded students. A good place to start looking is the Summer Schools and Summer Courses UK Directory (www.summer-schools.info). Some courses are residential, others are not. You should make the usual enquiries about CRB checks, adult-to-children ratios and supervision details.

> *All our children LOVED their music holiday courses. it was a great opportunity for them to make new friends, hear other players and work with new teachers. I think it helped them to grow both personally and as musicians!*
>
> Megan

Horn players at an NYO rehearsal. Photo © Kiran Ridely

National Youth Music Organisations

- ★ Music for Youth
- ★ National Youth Brass Band of Great Britain
- ★ National Youth Choirs of Great Britain
- ★ National Youth Jazz Collective
- ★ National Youth Orchestra of Great Britain
- ★ National South Asian Youth Orchestra
- ★ National Children's Orchestra of Great Britain
- ★ Youth Music Theatre: UK

Problems with progress

After the initial excitement of starting an instrument, your child might seem to lose interest in playing or get upset if you suggest that they practise. Before you cancel their lessons and sell their instrument on eBay, try these troubleshooting tips.

Is your child's instrument fit for purpose?

Has your child's instrument been correctly set up and is it in a playable state? The instrument will be uncomfortable to play if it isn't the correct size and if it needs maintenance it may be virtually unplayable. If the instrument is not fit for purpose this can be really demotivating and even stressful for your child, and they may end up blaming themselves for their lack of progress.

Info point

If you think there might be a problem with a school or music service/hub instrument that your child is borrowing, it is worth discussing this tactfully with your child's teacher as they may be able to arrange for the instrument to be serviced.

Is your child getting on with their teacher?

It may take a few months for your child and their teacher to get to know each other and find out what works best for them both. This may particularly be the case if your child is having short lessons or group lessons where they may not get so much time with the teacher. If your child really does not get on with their teacher, try and have a chat with the teacher first to see if this can be overcome. Often the problems do not lie so much in a clash of personalities, but in different tastes and possibly interests in genre and repertoire.

Is your child enjoying the music they are learning?

Finding pieces your child is passionate about and really wants to play can have very positive results. If you feel that your child isn't enjoying the repertoire that their teacher has chosen for them, it is worth chatting to the teacher and to see whether it would be possible to introduce some new pieces that reflect your child's musical tastes more closely. It might also be a good opportunity to discuss preferences of genre that were perhaps not touched upon when lessons were started, or which have developed subsequently.

Is your child with suitable co-learners in group lessons?

Children learning in groups will progress at different rates. If a child is left behind or is progressing much faster than their co-learners this can lead to frustration or boredom. Bring this up tactfully with the teacher (and not in front of the other children). An effective teacher should, within reason, be able to compensate for differing abilities in lessons and should be able to give your child extra exercises and pieces to learn at home to allow them to grow musically. Your teacher may also recommend that your child joins with another group of co-learners or extra activities, for example in a more advanced ensemble organised by their local music service/hub.

Is your child playing the right instrument for them?

Sometimes a child will simply not warm to a particular instrument as much as they thought they might. This situation is quite common and some of the world's most famous musicians have started on one instrument only to discover that their 'true calling' is with another! If you suspect that this is the case, your child's teacher may be able to recommend a new instrument or you could use the Instrument factfiles to choose an instrument with your child.

If your child changes instruments the initial lessons will not have been wasted, particularly if they choose another instrument within the same 'family'. The basic musical skills your child has acquired on their first instrument can be easily transferred to a second instrument and progress should be much swifter the second time around.

> I started on the bassoon – and I did like the sound, but the fingerings were confusing and I could not handle the thumb flick. I had the opportunity to try the trombone at school and I was just off! I got to grade 7 in two years!
>
> James, age 14

Is your child frustrated because they feel they are not getting better?

If your child feels frustrated and doesn't feel that they are making progress, it is a good idea to point out that learning a new skill takes a lot of time and that progress is not always obvious for a while (see the learning curve on p55). Work with your child's teacher to establish small but tangible goals that your child can work to and achieve.

Another reason your child may be struggling is that they may not be doing enough practice or they may not be practising efficiently. A good teacher will pick up on this and will have the confidence to discuss this with you. You can help by checking that your child understands what they should be practising and continue to remind them gently to practise, praise their achievements and listen to their playing. It is also worth checking that the practice book instructions from your child's teacher are clear. If your child is struggling to understand what they need to do at home it is worth raising this with their teacher.

Is your child anxious about failure?

Sometimes children can be anxious about failing. If your child has suddenly stopped practising, a fear of failure might be behind their sudden drop in motivation. They might feel that the repertoire has become too difficult, or that their peers are getting considerably better than them, so not trying at all might feel like the safest option. If this is the case you will need to discuss this with your child's teacher and try to find a solution to rebuild your child's confidence.

Another reason your child may be feeling inadequate or frustrated with their progress could be that they have been unfairly comparing themselves to their classmates. Explain to your child that the important thing is that they enjoy playing and continue to improve and that it doesn't matter how the other children are doing.

Is your child experiencing negative peer pressure?

Sometimes children can get teased, or even bullied, for playing an instrument that their peers don't consider to be 'cool'. If you think your child may be being bullied, report this to the school. If your child feels that they are missing out on time with their friends but would still like to practise, try and agree on a time, perhaps first thing in the morning, when practice won't interfere with socialising.

Is your child finding it difficult to fit their practice around schoolwork?

For many children, playing an instrument can be a welcome break from studying and it helps them relax. However, if your child has more homework and tests than usual and is finding it hard to cope, speak to your child's music teacher and explain that your child may not have as much time to dedicate to their practice as usual. Look at your child's day and see if you can help them to be more organised in order to fit more commitments in. If your child still feels really overburdened, for example in the run-up to their GCSEs, it might be time to stop music lessons for a bit.

Has your child simply lost interest?

As children get older and their horizons expand, they may find other activities they would rather pursue. Perhaps they have become really good at sport or art or they would prefer to spend more time with their friends. If your child really wants to stop there is not much point in forcing them to persist. You could encourage them to keep playing in an ensemble or choir and keep the option open of taking up lessons again at a later stage. After a break your child might find that they do miss playing their instrument after all.

Exams

Graded music exams are a great tool to motivate your child to practise and to measure progress but they aren't suitable for everyone. There are good arguments for and against exams, and you need to consider carefully whether exams are suitable for your child.

Why take exams?

Structured goals that inspire and motivate progress

Performance opportunities in a formal, yet sympathetic environment

Useful feedback from respected and independent musicians who have undergone rigorous training and are constantly monitored by a Chief Examiner using internationally recognised benchmarks

Confidence boost from having efforts validated by an independent examiner

Reassurance and formal acknowledgement and evidence of progress for hard work

When exams don't work

There are, of course, drawbacks associated with exams. Exams should never be the end goal for a musician and teachers should not teach solely 'to exams' as they are not a complete framework for learning. Another danger is that pupils are encouraged to take one exam after another, which is not advisable.

All musicians need to take time out from exams to play a variety of pieces in different styles and widen their musical horizons. Remember that having lessons is about making music both alone and with others rather than acquiring one exam certificate after the other.

In some cases, you may find that the negative factors, particularly nerves, outweigh all the positive benefits of taking exams. If your child really does not enjoy taking exams they might be happier performing music in less formal contexts instead and there is no point pressuring them to take exams.

Preparing for an exam

The teacher's role

Your child's teacher will usually suggest to you and your child that they are ready to take an exam. They will also need to check that your child is ready to practise hard and wants to succeed in the exam before entering them for it. A good teacher can gauge how long it will take to prepare for an exam and will discuss possible exam dates with you to check that your child will be available.

Once the exam date has been set, your child's teacher should help your child to pick the right pieces so that they enjoy preparing for the exam. This is a really important factor in exam success. They will also ensure that all aspects of the exam, including scales, sight-reading, and aural tests are regularly covered in lessons.

Nearer to the exam date, the teacher may arrange for performance opportunities, perhaps with other pupils and their parents, to prepare your child for a formal performance.

A lot of teachers arrange mock exams to allow the pupil to familiarise themselves with the format of the exams so there aren't any surprises. This also provides a good opportunity to see how a child reacts to pressure and to talk through any concerns they may have about performing.

Your role

Supporting and encouraging your child

Your main role as a parent is to provide all the support, encouragement and praise that your child needs. Overall, the best approach for a parent to take is to stay relaxed and upbeat throughout (this isn't always easy!). Remember to praise and reward your child for regular effort and practice as this is vital when preparing for an exam. If possible, try to be available as often as possible for performances at home that are initiated by your child and remember to praise and encourage even if you feel that the piece is not quite ready to be performed to an examiner.

 Info point

If your child keeps stopping when they make a mistake it is useful to remind them at the end of the performance that the mistakes they make are not as bad as they perceive them to be and that it is more important to keep playing.

Providing materials

When your child is preparing for an exam there are also a few material considerations. They will need repertoire books and it may be useful to buy scales books and aural practice books too, which they can use to practise at home. The exam itself needs to be paid for too; check with your child's teacher, use the exam board website or call the exam board to find this information.

Helping your child to be organised

✓ Check that your child's exam doesn't clash with any holidays or school trips.

✓ It isn't advisable to book a holiday just before an exam as your child may not then be able to practise during the important lead-up period.

✓ Remind your child that they need to do all the exercises that their teacher has asked them to do as they may avoid practising things that they are less comfortable with.

✓ Check with your child's teacher whether they will be providing the accompaniment during the exam. If they are unable to do this, you will need to book and pay for an accompanist. Your child's teacher may be able to recommend someone or you can contact your local music service/hub, music shop or exam centre for a list of recommended accompanists.

Things to avoid doing:

(!) Avoid making exams into a competitive target or as a way to compare your child to their peers – exams should be seen as a personal goal and a reflection of personal progress as well as an objective guide to what could be improved on.

(!) Try to avoid going into 'teacher mode' during the build-up to the exams. This will potentially create a more stressful situation for your child, which may result in them not wanting you to get involved in the future. It is best to leave constructive criticism up to the teacher; that is what you are paying them for.

The night before

It goes without saying that a good night's sleep can help your child stay calm and alert during their exam. Make sure they're in bed in good time with the minimum of distractions. If they don't sleep as well as they'd hoped, don't make a big deal of it and reassure them that it's only one night so they will be fine.

The day of the exam

What your child will need

The day of the big exam has finally arrived! Here is a list of everything (apart from the instrument and music) that you and your child will need to take to the exam:

- ✓ accessories (spare strings, rosin for strings players and spare reeds for woodwind players)

- ✓ the correct stationery if taking a written theory exam

- ✓ exam time and address.

Info point

Aim to arrive at least ten minutes before the exam is due to start and try and plan ahead for any traffic problems to reduce unnecessary stress.

When you arrive at the test centre a steward will register your child and will show them the waiting room. Usually there is also a warm-up room but time is often limited due to the number of candidates.

Tips on exam etiquette:

- Encourage your child to smile when they go into the exam room and to speak clearly and confidently when they address the examiner.

- Remind your child that it is fine to take their time and ensure that they are comfortable before the exam starts and that if they need help adjusting a music stand or a piano stool they shouldn't be afraid to ask the examiner.

- If your child is taking a piano exam, remind them that they are allowed to play a few bars of a piece or a scale to familiarise themselves with the feel of the piano.

Dealing with nerves

Nerves are part of every performer's life. Even professional musicians often feel nervous before performances.

Here are some useful nerve-busting tips:

- Encourage your child to concentrate on giving an enjoyable performance and try to enjoy playing.

- Remind your child that the examiner expects them to be a bit nervous so it is nothing to be ashamed of or concerned about. The examiner is on their side and wants to give them a good mark.

- Like all exams, a music exam is just a snapshot of one performance on one day. If your child doesn't get the mark that they hoped for this doesn't mean that they have 'failed' as a musician. Exams can always be retaken.

- Remind your child that the examiner may leave a short, silent pause after each part of the test. This is when the examiner is making notes so it is nothing to worry about. In fact, this could be a good opportunity for them to take some deep breaths and compose themselves if they're feeling nervous.

- Try and remain relaxed and positive yourself. Being stressed or putting on the pressure won't help your child's nerves.

> " I used to be really nervous before playing to other people, but I now play my piece at the end of my lesson for the next student and it has really helped me. I also play for my family whenever I can!
>
> Sam, 11

If you think that your child may struggle particularly with nerves, it may be worth having a chat with their teacher to see if they can work on this specifically. Their teacher will have almost certainly experienced nerves too so it may help for them to share their experience with your child. They should also be able to suggest some simple relaxation techniques that your child can practise in the run-up to the exam and use on the day to calm themselves down.

After the exam

After the exam, remember to praise and reward your child for their effort. They may feel tired and a bit downtrodden if they feel that the exam didn't go as well as they'd hoped. If your child gets upset, try to be cheerful and don't make too much of a deal about it. Reassure them that they should not just focus on their mistakes and that the examiner will mark the overall performance. It is also important to remind your child that the period after the exam is an exciting time when they will be able to start playing some new pieces and learn new skills. If you have concerns about how the exam went or if your child was particularly upset afterwards, it is a good idea to discuss this with your child's teacher.

The results

A few weeks later you will receive a letter with written feedback and a mark for your child's performance. Depending on the exam board, you may also be able to view the exam results online. Whatever the result, be positive about your child's effort and achievement. If you have any questions or are concerned about the mark awarded or the examiner's feedback, have a chat with your child's teacher.

Future exams

It is important that you don't push your child to move straight onto the next grade straight away as they need to enjoy music making without exam pressure. Should your child's progress take off, it is possible to skip a grade and your child's teacher will advise you on what they think should be the next step.

Exam boards

There is a bewildering choice of examinations on offer. Although your child's teacher should be aware of the different boards and will be able to recommend a suitable board for your child, it is still useful to know about the range of exams available.

Popular exam boards:

ABRSM: www.abrsm.org

Trinity Guildhall:
www.trinitycollege.co.uk

LCM: www.uwl.ac.uk

Rockschool: www.rockschool.co.uk

Exams for beginners

LCM Early Learning is an assessment for three to six year olds. The exams can be taken solo or in a group. The exams are conducted in a very relaxed environment and the teacher can be present. Candidates are awarded a Pass, Merit or Distinction and all children who complete the assessment are awarded at least a Pass.

LCM Steps are pre-Grade 1 exams in selected subjects. They are an ideal way to introduce pupils to examinations and provide a useful goal to work towards. Candidates receive a written report and mark, and successful candidates receive a certificate.

ABRSM Prep Test is for learners who have had around six to nine months of lessons. The test ensures that they have all the musical and technical foundations that they are needed for graded exams. The test is designed to be as relaxed and enjoyable as possible. No marks are awarded and there is no pass or fail. Each candidate is awarded a certificate and receives helpful and positive comments from the examiner.

Trinity Guildhall Initial is aimed at beginners who have had 6–9 months of lessons. All candidates are awarded a certificate. Be aware that it is not offered in all subjects.

ABRSM Music Medals

Music Medals are assessments and teaching resources designed to introduce musical skills and to encourage playing together. There are five levels: Copper, Bronze (beginners), Silver, Gold and Platinum (further musical progress). The assessments cover playing together, playing solo and musicianship skills. While group playing is part of the exam only one child is assessed per exam. All performances are video recorded, marked by the teacher and moderated by ABRSM. Successful candidates receive a certificate and a Music Medal. Music Medals can be more accessible for some candidates due to the flexibility of supporting tests and repertoire choice.

Graded exams

Many exam boards, including all the main exam boards offer music exams for a wide range of instruments through a progressive system of eight levels and beyond. Marking is carefully moderated and the levels are recognised internationally. Most exam boards follow a similar structure and the examination pieces on each syllabus for each grade are roughly the same difficulty.

To progress to Grades 6–8 on the ABRSM syllabus your child will need to pass either the Grade 5 (or above) in Theory of Music, Practical Musicianship or any Grade 5 (or above) on any solo jazz instrument. All ABRSM, LCM and Trinity Guildhall graded exams are accredited and Grades 6–8 benefit from UCAS points which can be used as part of a university or college application in the UK.

Performance-only exams

Performance-only exams do not include an assessment of technical work or any supporting tests. There is a good range of performance-only exams available from the main exam boards:

- Music Certificates (Trinity Guildhall)
- **Performance awards (LCM):** these are assessed by DVD submission and can be taken at any time of the year
- Leisure Play (LCM)

Ensemble exams

Exam boards such as ABRSM, LCM and Trinity Guildhall offer exams for ensemble groups as well as individual musicians. The types of ensembles that are assessed can range from duos and trios to jazz ensembles, rock bands, folk groups, choirs and even orchestras and concert bands.

Theory exams

Theory exams are offered by most exam boards at Grades 1–8. If your child is taking graded exams on the ABRSM syllabus, they will need to pass either the Grade 5 (or above) in Theory of Music, Practical Musicianship or Grade 5 (or above) on any solo jazz instrument before progressing to the instrumental Grades 6–8. Regardless of whether an exam board requires Grade 5 theory, theory exams can be valuable way to gain a solid understanding of the building blocks of music and will also ultimately help your child with their playing. All ABRSM, LCM and Trinity Guildhall theory exams are accredited and Grades 6–8 benefit from UCAS points which can be used as part of a university or college application in the UK.

Graded rock exams

Trinity Guildhall rock and pop exams
(www.trinityrock.com)

Trinity Guildhall offers exams in bass, drums, guitar, keyboards and vocals from Initial grade to Grade 8 and Diploma level. The exams offer an alternative approach to the learning and teaching of rock and pop instruments. They have been designed to reflect the way rock and pop musicians learn, and to develop skills and techniques specific to rock and pop music. The exams consist of three songs (including a technical focus song and the option for the candidate to play a self-chosen song) and session skills (playback or improvising). Candidates are marks on fluency and musical detail, technical control, and communication and style.

Trinity Guildhall also offers a rock and pop group exam where bands of two or more players can play a set. One song must be specified by the exam board but the rest are chosen by the band and can include their own music. The band is marked on the same criteria as individual candidates. Bands can achieve a Foundation, Intermediate or Advanced certificate. All the exams are marked by a top quality panel of examiners and are fully accredited by Ofqual.

Rockschool (www.rockschool.co.uk)

Rockschool offers grade examinations and performance certificates for rock musicians. Rockschool graded exams run from Entry Level, through Grades 1 to 8. At each grade, there are two types of exams: Grade Exams and Performance Certificates. Grade Exams include three performance pieces, technical exercises and and musicianship tests and Performance Certificates consist of five performance pieces only. Band exams are also available at Grades 3, 5 and 8 for guitar, bass and drums and consist of five performance pieces. Rockschool exam pieces are performed to a backing CD to simulate a real live band environment. All exams are acredited and Grades 6–8 benefit from UCAS points.

Registry of Guitar Tutors Exams
(www.rgt.org)

The Registry of Guitar Tutors offers exams in electric, rock, acoustic, jazz, classical and bass guitar in partnership with the London College of Music Exams. The exams range from Preliminary Grade through to Grade 1 and up to Grade 8. Scales and arpeggios, chords, rhythm playing, lead playing, spoken tests and aural assessment. For Grades 6–8 there is an addition module of a specialism. All exams are acredited and Grades 6–8 benefit from UCAS points.

Teacher-assessed graded exams

MTB exams (www.mtbexams.com)

MTB is a music teachers' board providing a new way to take instrumental exams for MTB levels 1–8. The board uses the GCSE coursework model where the exams are assessed by the teacher and moderated by MTB. They aim to reduce stress levels for pupils and teachers, to offer complete flexibility over exams dates and are marked by specialist examiners.

Exam syllabuses

Exam syllabuses are usually easily downloadable from the internet or can be ordered as a hard copy from the exam board. Some exam syllabuses are available in music shops and are usually free. Grade examinations usually consist of repertoire pieces plus additional tests in aural, scales and sight-reading. There are usually several different 'lists' to choose from, each with a different style of music so there is plenty of choice on offer.

It's only an exam!

Failing a music exam is really not a big deal. Like all exams a grade exam is a snapshot of one performance on one day. Many things can and do go wrong. Additionally there are always external factors, which can have a negative impact on your child's performance, maybe your child is not feeling well on the day, maybe there were additional demands at school during exam week, maybe a beloved hamster has gone to the big hamster-run in the sky. Remember it's only an exam!

Performing

Most musicians regard public performances as the pay-off for their hard work and relish the chance to share their music making with others. Nothing quite beats the thrill of giving a well-received performance to an appreciative public, either as a soloist or with an ensemble. However, the excitement that comes with performing is sometimes combined with nerves and even self-doubt, even for the most seasoned performers. For many musicians, this powerful cocktail of emotions is what both attracts them to performing and can sometimes put them off wanting to play in public.

> It's really scary just before I perform but I like singing for other people because they enjoy listening. It makes me feel good because they always say nice things afterwards and that makes me happy and feel that it was worth the scary bit. My teacher taught me that music is about sharing and I like to share.
>
> Anna, age 9

Why perform?

Working towards a performance can be an incredibly motivating experience for your child and has the potential to propel their playing to a new level. It takes courage to perform in front of an audience and the self-confidence your child will gain from performing music will be useful for them in many other settings, from giving a presentation at school to public speaking in later life. It is also inspiring to hear other musicians perform and to take inspiration from potentially unknown repertoire and different interpretations of pieces by more advanced students. As your child progresses, more and more opportunities for performance will present themselves, and you should encourage your child to make the most of them.

Types of performance opportunities:

Formal:

★ exams

★ competitions

★ festivals

★ school concerts

★ assemblies

★ youth orchestra/ensemble concerts.

Informal opportunities:

★ playing during a service at your local church

★ community event

★ old people's homes

★ family and friends.

Demonstrating independence

A musical performance given for an audience is a special experience for a musician. It is in some respects one of the few occasions when your child needs to 'go it alone' without help from their parents or teacher. It is a valuable lesson in preparation, overcoming potential anxieties and giving an enjoyable performance.

Festivals

There are many local art and music festivals organised all over the UK, often run by charities who recognise the importance of giving performance opportunities to youngsters and amateurs as a vital part of nurturing and promoting musical culture. Your child's teacher should be informed about such opportunities and it is a good idea to encourage your child to take part in these festivals. The festival landscape is constantly changing and evolving, but you should be able to find information in your local library, the British Music Yearbook (Rhinegold Publishing) and online.

How to prepare for a performance

A successful performance depends on thorough preparation. Your child's teacher needs to work with your child on all three aspects of a successful performance:

● technique

● interpretation

● stagecraft.

Technique

It almost goes without saying that your child will have worked hard on playing all the right notes in the right order! If your child is unable to play through the piece without stopping or making a mistake at home, then you can safely assume that the piece is not ready for performance and that in most likelihood things will go wrong on the platform.

Interpretation

Performance is not about technical perfection; it is about conveying emotions and being expressive. Just as actors bring different insights to their part, a musical performer will have their own ideas on how to perform a piece. Aspects to consider are

- **tempo** (how fast, where to slow down a little, etc.)
- **dynamics** (when to play loudly and quietly)
- **phrasing** (how to divide a musical line and where to put the emphasis)
- **style** (to apply the above criteria consistently and in keeping with the period the piece was written).

In many ways it can be preferable to have a technically flawed but emotional and musical performance, rather than a robotic reproduction delivered without feeling.

Stagecraft

It is important that your teacher works with your child on stagecraft as this will help your child deliver a more confident performance.

Your child may have plenty of questions such as:

? How do I walk on and off stage?

? Where should I stand?

? Should I smile?

? Should I introduce the piece to the audience?

? How do I indicate to the accompanist that I'm ready to start playing?

? What should I do if my part has rests, but the accompanist is still playing?

? What happens if I need to start again?

The more familiar your child is with the answers to these questions the better, as it will take away extraneous concerns for your child and allow them to concentrate solely on their performance.

It is important that your child also looks the part as this will boost their confidence and get them in the right frame of mind to perform. Make sure you ask their teacher what the dress code is for the performance, in particular if it is an ensemble event as your child won't want to stick out.

 Info point

Keep calm and carry on!

As mentioned in the chapter on exams, things can and do go wrong on stage. When they do, the best course of action is to smile and carry on as if nothing has happened. Your child will be surprised how many members of the audience won't have noticed anything untoward!

Nerves and keeping performances in perspective!

A little nervous excitement before a performance can actually be desirable as it shows that your child is taking the occasion seriously. The art is for your child to tap into that extra bit of energy to deliver a vibrant performance. Younger children are normally less self-conscious than teenagers, and when discussing 'nerves' be careful how you broach the topic, as you don't want to give a perfectly at ease six-year-old the idea that they should be feeling nervous.

At the venue

Discuss with your child's teacher whether going on and off stage has been practised at the venue and if your child needs any help setting up on stage. This includes tuning, carrying the instrument and music stand etc.

Mock performances

If your child is very nervous, try to arrange little 'mock' performances at home in front of family and friends, neighbours etc. The more your child is used to performing, the less of a big deal it will become. You should also remind your child that audiences are very appreciative of young people's efforts and that they don't expect Carnegie Hall-level professional performances.

Don't force your child to perform

If your child is too distressed by the idea of performing, do not force them. Give them time to warm to the idea of performing in public and encourage them to carry on doing mini performances to encouraging family members in the meantime to build their confidence.

After the performance

After a successful performance, musicians usually feel a mixture of elation and pride and positive comments will be very much appreciated. If your child feels that their performance hasn't gone to plan, it is even more important to be positive and to focus on the effort which has gone into the preparation. Remind your child that even professional musicians are not always happy with their performances. Try and encourage your child to perform again as soon as the opportunity arises so that they don't start to see performing as a negative experience.

Professional associations and societies

Music Industries Association (MIA):
www.mia.org.uk

National Association of Music Educators
(NAME): **www.name.org.uk**

Federation of Music Services (FMS):
www.thefms.org

Musicians' Union (MU):
www.musiciansunion.org.uk and
www.musicteachers.co.uk

The Incorporated Society of Musicians (ISM):
www.ism.org

Registry of Guitar Tutors: **www.rgt.org**

European Guitar Teachers Association:
www.egta.co.uk

Association of Teachers of Singing:
www.aotos.org.uk

British Flute Society: **www.bfs.org.uk**

Flutewise: **www.flutewise.com**

Clarinet and Saxophone Society:
www.cassgb.org

European Recorder Teacher's Association:
www.erta.org.uk

Trombone Society:
www.trombone-society.org.uk

Early learning/musicianship methods

British Suzuki Institute:
www.britishsuzuki.org.uk

The British Kodály Academy:
www.britishkodalyacademy.org

The Dalcroze Society: **www.dalcroze.org.uk**

Centres of Advanced Training

www.education.gov.uk (search for 'Centres for
Advanced Training')

Instrument purchasing advice

MIA: downloadable PDF on Purchasing a
Quality Instrument. Also available in hard
copy: **www.mia.org.uk/publications**

Guitar: **www.firstguitar.com**

Saxophone: **www.shwoodwind.co.uk**

Instrument Buyers Guide (free downloadable
guide by Rhinegold Publishing):
www.rhinegold.co.uk